GREAT MILITARY LEADERS

Hannibal

Joel Newsome

Cavendish Square

Published in 2018 by Cavendish Square Publishing, LLC
243 5th Avenue, Suite 136, New York, NY 10016

First Edition

Website: cavendishsq.com

Library of Congress Cataloging-in-Publication Data

Names: Newsome, Joel, author.
Title: Hannibal / Joel Newsome.
Description: New York : Cavendish Square Publishing, [2018] | Series: Great military leaders | Includes bibliographical references and index.
Identifiers: LCCN 2017000940 (print) | LCCN 2017001560 (ebook) | ISBN 9781502628695 (library bound) | ISBN 9781502628701 (E-book)
Subjects: LCSH: Hannibal, 247 B.C.-182 B.C.--Juvenile literature. | Punic War, 2nd, 218-201 B.C.--Juvenile literature. | Generals--Tunisia--Carthage (Extinct city)--Biography--Juvenile literature. | Rome--History--Republic, 265-30 B.C.--Juvenile literature. | Carthage (Extinct city)--History--Juvenile literature.
Classification: LCC DG249 .N49 2018 (print) | LCC DG249 (ebook) | DDC 937/.04092 [B] --dc23
LC record available at https://lccn.loc.gov/2017000940

Editorial Director: David McNamara
Editor: Molly Fox
Copy Editor: Rebecca Rohan
Associate Art Director: Amy Greenan
Designer: Jessica Nevins
Production Coordinator: Karol Szymczuk
Photo Research: J8 Media

The photographs in this book are used by permission and through the courtesy of: Cover Leemage/Universal Images Group/Getty Images; p. 4 Paris Louvre/Alamy Stock Photo; p. 8 Irina Burakova/Shutterstock.com; p. 10-11 Dorling Kindersley/Thinkstock; p. 15 tingra/iStock; p. 17 Internet Archive Book Images/Wikimedia Commons/File:Naval battles, ancient and modern (1883) (14578299319).jpg/CC PD; p. 20-21 Marzolino/Shutterstock.com; p. 25 Kritzolina/Wikimedia Commons/File:Mosaik der Tanit in Kerkouane, Tunesien Januar 2015.jpg/CC BY-SA 4.0; p. 30 Winfield Parks/National Geographic/Getty Images; p. 37 Timothy R. Nichols/Shutterstock.com; p. 38, 84 Look and Learn/Bridgeman Images; p. 40 Carole Raddato/Wikimedia Commons/File:Hannibal bust Cartagena.jpg/CC BY-SA 2.0; p. 45 Millionstock.com/Shutterstock.com; p. 48 Kean Collection/Archive Photos/Getty Images; p. 50 Ipsumpix/Corbis Historical/Getty Images; p. 53 Carlos/Wikimedia Commons/File:Ebro river he map.svg/CC BY-SA 4.0; p. 56 Abalg/Wikimedia Commons/File:Hannibal route of invasion-en.svg/CC BY-SA 3.0; p. 64 MagentaGreen/Wikimedia Commons/File:Battle of Lake Trasimene.svg/CC BY-SA 4.0; p. 68-69 North Wind Picture Archives/Alamy Stock Photo; p. 70 Johnny Shumate/Wikimedia Commons/File:Balearic Slinger.jpg/CC PD; p. 74 Hulton Archive/Getty Images; p. 79 PHAS/Universal Images Group/Getty Images; p. 82 Mohammad Adil/Wikimedia Commons/File:Mohammad adil rais-battle of zama-1.PNG/CC BY-SA 3.0; p. 89 Bob Thomas/Popperfoto/Getty Images; p. 92 Chronicle/Alamy Stock Photo; p. 96 INTERFOTO/Alamy Stock Photo; p. 100-101 Time Life Pictures/The LIFE Picture Collection/Getty Images; p. 103 Ian Dagnall/Alamy Stock Photo; p. 109 Hans Casparius/Hulton Archive/Getty Images; p. 112 Stefano Bianchetti/Corbis Historical/Getty Images.

Printed in the United States of America

TABLE OF CONTENTS

ANIBAL CA

INTRODUCTION

Throughout recorded time, military leaders have risen to prominence through a variety of means. Some are experts at strategy, some are fierce warriors in battle, and others are highly skilled in the ways of reconnaissance. The best leaders display a well-rounded skill set both in **diplomacy** and dominance. These warriors are able to lift their people up as they make their mark on the pages of history. Some of these leaders have had their exploits well documented while others have all but disappeared from memory. This text will explore a great general who, while very little trace of his people remains with us today, has lived on as a legendary strategist and fighter. His methods, bravery, and charisma allowed him to march through foreign territories recruiting men to his cause, cross treacherous terrain that other leaders thought impassable, and become Rome's most formidable and hated enemy. His very name struck fear into the hearts of Romans. Hannibal Barca lived his life with the single-minded focus of bringing death to Rome. This mission, handed down from his father, another great general, would so define his life that the Second Punic War that he waged is often referred to as the Hannibalic War. The fact that the wars between Carthage, Hannibal's homeland, and Rome are referred to as Punic is a testament to the fact that history is written by those that are victorious. While Hannibal accomplished impressive feats and triumphed in key battles while fighting Rome, he was unable to

Opposite: This bronze medallion features what some believe to be a representation of Hannibal's profile.

win the war, and Carthage was eventually destroyed. Punic is an ancient slur used to refer to the Carthaginians and their ancestors, the Phoenicians.

Phoenicia was a conglomerate of independent city-states situated on the eastern coast of the Mediterranean. The Phoenicians made their living through trade and were aggressively competitive with each other as well as other traders. Phoenicia was fully established around 1500 BCE and fell to Alexander the Great in 332 BCE. The feisty maritime spirit of the coalesced city-states was handed down to Carthage, which was established by citizens fleeing the city of Tyre. Meanwhile, Rome was fighting to expand its territory in Italy. While Carthage was primarily known for its navy and sea trade, its most famous son spent his life waging war on land.

Hannibal's father, Hamilcar, fought in the First Punic War and returned home bitter about the surrender of Carthage. Hannibal would have grown up in this post-war climate, listening to his father's stories about the despised Roman Republic. As soon as Hamilcar was able to, he journeyed to Iberia (modern-day Spain) with troops in order to restore Carthage's wealth and military power. He brought his three sons, Mago, Hasdrubal, and Hannibal along, thus beginning Hannibal's life of military discipline.

Hannibal's incredible victories are testaments to his impeccable strategies, reconnaissance, and multinational army that featured a diverse set of soldiers that the Romans had to contend with. His victories, the Battle of Cannae in particular, have been studied by military academies, history enthusiasts, and schoolchildren alike. His name and deeds are echoed in novels, poetry, paintings, films, and other art forms, as the myth of

Hannibal continues to change with time while still captivating even modern audiences.

For all that we know of this great leader, there is still so much that we do not and will probably never know of the real Hannibal Barca. The total annihilation of Carthage erased any direct information from the culture, and historians have had to depend on accounts of Hannibal and his life written by Greeks and Romans, societies that have traditionally denigrated him and his homeland. Nevertheless, the work of Polybius, Livy and other ancient Roman and Greek writers have allowed a fractured picture of Hannibal to emerge. Still, modern scholars remain perplexed by Hannibal's accomplishments and ultimate failure. How did he manage to cross the French Alps? Where was his crossing made? Why didn't he attempt to seize Rome after the Battle of Cannae? Why did he continue his onslaught even after defeat seemed imminent? We may never know the answers to these pertinent inquiries, but scientists and scholars continue to ponder and investigate Hannibal's life and work.

The following chapters will offer a glimpse into what we know of Hannibal Barca and how he went about fighting the massive Roman army. Carthage's history and culture will be explored as well as Hannibal's lasting legacy, how the mythology surrounding his quest has developed and evolved, and how Rome and the world changed as a result of doing battle with the much-feared Hannibal Barca.

CHAPTER ONE

The Culture *of* Carthage

Hannibal Barca was born a citizen of the city-state Carthage, located on the North coast of Africa. The city was a major, multinational trading hub, and its powerful navy and its innovative use of technological advancements were well known across the Mediterranean. Though many admired the growing city, its riches and enviable position eventually made it a target for formidable opponents.

Carthage's Ancestors

In order to understand Carthage and its influence on the ancient world, the culture of the Phoenicians must be examined. Phoenicia was a group of independent city-states established along the coast of the Mediterranean. It was composed of the lands we now know as Syria, Lebanon, and parts of Israel. As a result of their location, Phoenicians were a **seafaring** people. They excelled at shipbuilding, mass manufacturing, and maritime trade, and thrived between the years of 1500 and 322 BCE.

Opposite: These ancient ruins are all that's left of the great city-state of Carthage.

This map illustrates the ancient empire of Phoenicia and the established trade routes that brought the civilization to power.

The name Phoenicia is derived from the ancient Greek word *phoínios*, which means purple. The region's name came from the fact that they used purple dye to color the robes of Mesopotamian royalty. The Greek historian, Herodotus, tells us that Phoenicia was also responsible for creating the alphabet, delivered to Greece by a Phoenician prior to the 8th century BCE. The majority of modern western languages take their foundation from the Phoenician alphabet. This ancient grouping of peoples on the

Mediterranean was also responsible for exporting **papyrus**, the ancient form of paper, to the Greeks and the Egyptians. Without the Phoenicians, it is uncertain what path the history of language would have taken. Though they were instrumental in the initiation of written record, it is believed that the Phoenicians also handed down spiritual beliefs to their ancient neighbors. Historians have acknowledged striking similarities between the Greek gods Zeus and Poseidon when compared with Phoenician deities Baal and Yamm.

In the Biblical book of Ezekiel, the Phoenicians are appropriately referred to as "princes of the sea." Known for their sailing ability and ship construction expertise, and as architects of various trade routes, they certainly must have seemed like maritime royalty. In fact, they are responsible for the invention of the curved **hull,** which originated in the Phoenician city-state Byblos. Because they were such highly skilled sailors and could navigate the oftentimes turbulent Mediterranean, Phoenicians became efficient transporters of goods. They specialized in transferring luxury items and bulk raw materials from a variety of international markets back to Western Asia. Phoenician seamen traveled to areas that were relatively close, such as Greece, Cyprus, and Egypt, but also as far as places like modern-day Britain and Mesopotamia. These newly established trade routes allowed the region to prosper in terms of wealth and cultural exchange. Archaeologists have studied Phoenician shipwrecks and seen the variety of cargo that these ancient people transported. Containers that are believed to have carried exotic balms, wine, and oils, as well as glass, gold, silver, copper, tin, pottery supplies and other treasures, were discovered. In addition to goods and materials, Phoenicians also transported culture throughout the ancient world. Modern historians consider them great intermediaries in the exchange of social customs. The expanse of Phoenician trade routes, their expert sailing, and the value of the goods they transported meant that they rarely suffered from foreign invasion. Military powers generally left the Phoenicians to conduct trade, as they were able to foster wealth among a variety of regions; however, their seafaring **prowess** and growing wealth were the envy of other ancient cultures.

Carthaginians are descendent from residents of Tyre, the most prosperous city in Phoenicia. Competition within Phoenicia for accumulated riches and power was highly valued. Tyre made a lucrative alliance with Israel in the early days of the kingdom that allowed the city-state to accumulate massive wealth for itself and its citizens while the rest of Phoenicia struggled to keep up. Ancient myth places the time of Carthage's founding around 814 BCE, but it is now believed that Carthage was founded as a result of Alexander the Great's invasion and subsequent conquering of Tyre in 332 BCE.

Birth of Carthage

While Carthage did grow into a multinational metropolis, it began as a small seaport used as a Phoenician trading post for ship repair and supply. After the fall of Tyre, those that could escape the wrath of Alexander the Great, either through bribery or by stealth, escaped to Carthage. Tyrians who managed to reach Carthage were very wealthy and set about establishing Carthage as the new center of Mediterranean trade. Once the new residents arrived, they drove native inhabitants from the land, and then enslaved or severely taxed those that remained. In less than a century, Carthage grew from a small town to an enormous city that spread out for miles, the richest in all the Mediterranean. Just as the Phoenicians before them, Carthaginians set about establishing new trade routes and territories to fuel the growing city's fortune. The wealth accumulated from trade was supplemented by **tariffs** that regularly increased the city's affluence. Prosperous aristocrats were housed in palaces, while less wealthy residents lived in unassuming, well-built homes. The wealth of Carthage drew people from all over the world, and the city's population swelled to over three hundred thousand people. The task of housing and protecting the growing population was embraced with a distinct spirit of ingenuity characteristic of Carthage.

Engineering

Like their ancestors, Carthaginians were known for their engineering feats. Many of Hannibal's future accomplishments would not have been possible without the foundation of Carthaginian engineering. The Mediterranean seafarers would revolutionize the way city inhabitants were housed. They improved upon the shipbuilding of their **predecessors** and constructed an immense harbor which held its impressive fleet. Travelers who approached Carthage could plainly see how astounding their construction achievements were. The city was completely surrounded, encased by massive walls.

Walls of Carthage

The immense walls of Carthage formed a protective perimeter around the city. These walls stretched a circumference of twenty-three miles (thirty-seven kilometers) and comprised a three-part system that shielded the residents from outside forces. The first layer of defense was a ditch backed by a low wall that was packed with soil. The low wall was typically patrolled by a front line of soldiers. The relatively small wall was enough protection to allow the soldiers protection in the event of an assault and the ability to quickly withdraw in the event of an encroaching enemy. The second layer of resistance was a middle stone wall, taller than the first low wall but dwarfed in comparison to the third component of the perimeter. The final and most impressive fortification was a mammoth stone wall that stood 45 feet (13.8 meters) high and was at least 30 feet (9.1 m) wide at its most narrow point. The

These ruins stand on the grounds of what was once the site of the city-state Carthage.

inner wall featured fifteen towers which were placed at 200-yard (183 m) intervals. Watchmen stood guard in these towers and were able to alert authorities should anything on the horizon seem amiss.

Apartment Buildings

With a steadily increasing population, Carthaginian builders were forced to find ways to house the city's stream of new residents. As the challenge of housing grew more and more pressing, Carthage looked to the sky. The answer to providing resident housing took the form of ancient apartment buildings. Carthaginians harvested limestone from the Mediterranean basin and began constructing towering domiciles that reached six stories high. Modern archaeologists believe that Carthaginians cut the limestone into uniform, level blocks much like the Egyptians had before them. A simple cut would've been pounded into the limestone with a sharp rock. A piece of wood would then be wedged into the carved impression. Once the wood was placed, it was soaked with water, and as the bloated wood expanded, the stone would crack in almost perfect lines. The formed blocks of limestone would then be shipped to the building site and assembled.

Indoor Plumbing

Not only were Carthaginians able to house the city's robust population, those residing behind its protective walls enjoyed the convenience of indoor plumbing. Though domestic plumbing was present in predated civilizations, Carthage was the first to construct a unified system of water delivery and sewage disposal. Carthaginians used **cisterns** that were constructed of two layers of eggshell, clay and ash, which made the containers completely watertight. Residences had access to cisterns through a series of rudimentary pipes and channels that supplied the city with fresh running water. The city's inhabitants enjoyed fully functional bathrooms with bathtubs, sinks, and even showers, years before ancient Rome did.

Ships

Probably the best-known engineering feat of the Carthaginians was their shipbuilding. Again, they capitalized on the accomplishments of those that had come before them. Hundreds

Romans learned to design quinqueremes by studying wrecked Carthaginian ships.

of ships were constructed using mass-produced parts that were marked for placement during assembly. These mass-production methods allowed Carthaginian ships to be quickly replenished in times of warfare, adding to the strength of the forceful navy. These massive warships were constructed using oak, pine and fir woods, propelled by rows of oarsmen along with sails, and made to both withstand and deal considerable blows.

The Phoenicians had introduced the **trireme**, a huge battleship featuring three tiers of rowers with three men per oar. In the fourth century BCE, Carthage improved upon Phoenician design, building bigger and faster ships. The **quinquereme** was a result of Carthaginian innovation. Designed to be fast and maneuverable, the quinquereme featured three levels of rowers comprised of five rowers per oar. The warships are colossal, measuring 120 feet (36.6 m) long and anywhere from 9 to 16 feet (2.7 to 4.9 m) wide. The vessels could hold up to four hundred and twenty sailors, and when they were fully loaded, they weighed in at around 100 tons (90.7 metric tons). This increase in size and manpower made the ships incredibly swift in the water and also very lethal. The ships were used not just for transport but as weapons. They were outfitted with large battering rams made of bronze, which were mounted on the prow just below the waterline. While the trireme was built to engage enemy ships, the massive quinqueremes were meant to hit the enemy once, sink the assaulted ship, and move to the next attack.

Carthage employed assembly lines to replenish the fleet using mass-produced pieces. This allowed Carthage to continually defend itself even when the huge battleships were sunk. The ability to regularly replace these giant weapons frustrated and overwhelmed their enemies in naval warfare. Ironically, this easy assembly ended up assisting Carthage's most powerful opponent. During the First Punic War, Rome was confounded by the constant barrage of the Carthage navy until Roman sailors discovered a wrecked quinquereme. By studying the design of the wrecked ship, the Romans were able to reverse-engineer the giant warship and eventually began assembling their own fleet, though they were not as well made as the Carthaginian originals.

Harbor

According to Polybius, Carthage had a fleet of around three hundred and fifty ships in 256 BCE. The mass proliferation of naval warships demanded that Carthaginians have an adequate harbor to store their fleet. In the second century BCE, Carthage had developed its harbor into the most advanced maritime facility in the world. Much like its impressive fortified perimeter, the expanse of the accommodating Carthaginian harbor could be seen from the seas of the Mediterranean. It made the Carthaginian way of life possible, as it was used for both military and commercial pursuits. The entrance to the harbor measured around seventy feet wide. It was outfitted with iron chains that allowed it to open and close alternately, allowing the fleet to move swiftly out to sea and sealing off enemies from accessing their port. Behind the iron chains, there were two separate **marinas**. The first was used for the ships of traders and was constructed for ease of loading and unloading goods in order to give trade a speedy efficiency. The second marina was located past the commercial marina and housed military vessels. The harbor was circular with thirty symmetrical docks located in the center of the circle. An additional one hundred and forty docks radiated out from its center, lining the perimeter. The entire harbor could accommodate an astounding two hundred and twenty ships.

Government

Though the Carthaginians typically honored and improved the structure of Phoenician society, they did not choose to rely solely on a monarch to govern the people as Phoenicia had. Carthage and its government were dominated by elite aristocratic clans. These exclusive groups held every crucial governmental and military position. The government was organized into a popular assembly of citizens who then elected members of the aristocracy to key positions. Participation in politics and government was reserved only for those who could claim citizenship: free, native men. While the general structure of the Carthaginian government is clear, some of the specific mechanics of government decisions

This illustration is an interpretation of what the harbor of ancient Carthage may have looked like.

have been obscured by the surviving Greek and Roman descriptions that apply their distinct terminology to describe politics in Carthage.

Suffetes

Starting in the fifth century BCE, the most influential position in Carthaginian politics was that of **suffete**. The office was shared by two suffetes, elected annually. It is believed that Carthage may have initially limited the position to one individual, but as Carthaginians became engaged in an increasing number of conflicts, the office was split. One was tasked with heading the military forces in times of war, while the other was responsible for government operations at home. They are believed to have operated in conjunction with the senate and also dealt with civil disputes. Status and wealth were prerequisites for being suitable for the office of suffete. After losing the Second Punic War, Hannibal returned to Carthage and held this office.

Senate

How influential Carthaginians were elected to the senate is unknown, but we do know that they served in these roles for life. It is believed that Carthage's senate was comprised of two to three hundred members. They were consulted by the suffetes on matters of government policy including military and financial issues. If the two government bodies could not reach a unanimous decision, the citizen's assembly would cast a deciding vote. This also occurred if there was dissent between the suffetes. There is conclusive evidence that the senate made decisions regarding war declaration, the deployment of military reinforcements, penalties for military leaders who failed in battle, and the acceptance of any conditions for peace offered by an enemy. Though a balance of power was attempted when governing on Carthage's soil, senators acted autonomously when traveling outside of Carthage.

Corruption

Government positions in Carthage were elected and, other than the senate, top positions featured term limits. Regular elections to limited term positions were probably instituted to ensure that individuals did not attain too much power. However, it seems corruption ran rampant in Carthaginian politics. It was common practice for a bribe to be offered in return for votes, eligibility for more powerful positions, and even favorable judgment in court. Corruption was such an issue that when Hannibal began his political career as a suffete upon returning to Carthage, he focused on easing the burden that corruption had placed on city finances. It is believed that one of the reasons Carthaginian politics was so plagued by abuse of power is the lack of compensation for serving as an official.

Religion

After the Third Punic War and Rome's destruction of ancient Carthage, many aspects of Carthaginian culture were lost to history. While we know Carthage had specific religious practices, modern historians have only been able to piece together what these practices may have been through the records of ancient Greek and Roman historians, many of whom looked down on foreign spirituality and referred to Carthaginian religious practice with terms from their own cultures. There are no surviving temples, only ruins. There are no texts that have been penned by Carthaginians themselves. Most of the information gathered directly from Carthage comes from surviving artifacts and inscriptions. Archaeologists have explored Carthaginian tombs and found masks and other objects that suggest the people of Carthage believed in some kind of life after death. However, the mythology surrounding their version of the afterlife can only be guessed at.

It is believed that there was a class of priests in Carthage. Much like the offices of government, eligibility for priesthood seems to have been determined by heredity and wealth. We know that the priests had a function in government, and that there were female priests, but their exact duties are something of a mystery. Inscriptions have taught modern people much of what we know about Carthage's priesthood. For instance, we know that there was a chief priest assigned to each temple, and each of them supervised a group of lower priests. Some historians think that priests were responsible for education in Carthage and may have been in charge of the libraries that are known to have existed in Carthage prior to its destruction by the Romans.

Inscriptions on Carthaginian artifacts are all we have to piece together our knowledge of temples in the great city-state. These inscriptions make mention of a variety of temples to many different gods, though only ruins remain. Historians guess that Carthage had about as many temples as existed in Rome and Athens. It is believed that these temples were similar in design and construction to Phoenician temples and that offerings were made at a designated altar.

Gods

Like their shipbuilding skills and trade practices, Carthage adopted much of their religious beliefs and practices from their ancestors, the Phoenicians. Like Phoenicia, Carthage maintained

polytheistic beliefs, meaning that they believed in more than one god. Carthage continued to worship Phoenician gods such as Melqart and Baal and also began to honor new gods such as Tanit. Like other aspects of Mediterranean culture, the belief in these different gods spread across the region along with trade and other cultural practices. The Carthaginians were steadfast in their devotion to the deities; their gods were honored with temples and ceremonies, their images were used to adorn currency and art, and there were even human sacrifices offered in appeasement.

One of the most important gods that Carthage inherited from Phoenicia was Melqart. Melqart was said to be the protector of the city of Tyre, and he is believed to have served the same role in Carthage. Surviving records suggest that colonists were required to offer a tenth of their annual earnings to the temple of Melqart in Tyre during the first centuries of Carthage's existence. When Hannibal was nine years old, he swore to Melqart that he would be an enemy of Rome for as long as he lived. Baal was another Phoenician god worshipped by Carthaginians. There is some confusion as to what Baal was meant to represent because there are many recorded names associated with this god. He was

This mosaic in modern day Tunisia honors the most important goddess in ancient Carthage: Tanit, a goddess of fertility.

worshipped as the supreme god in the Phoenician city of Sidon, and many historians believe Baal was somehow associated with Melqart. Other important Phoenician deities passed down to Carthage included Reshef (a god of warfare), Esmun (a healing deity), Hawot (god of the dead), and Semes (sun goddess).

The most important deity in Carthage was unique to the new city. Tanit, the goddess of fertility, became the most-worshipped deity around the fifth century BCE. She was inextricably linked to Baal and was often referenced as 'Tanit, face of Baal.' The symbol of Tanit is a triangle with a circle sitting on its top, a horizontal line runs between the triangle and circle. The symbol seems to be a rudimentary representation of a female figure with outstretched arms. It appears alongside inscriptions, in mosaics, on pottery, and on **stelae** (ancient stone slabs often serving as gravestones). While Tanit's symbol appears on a variety of surviving objects, no other symbols of Carthaginian gods have been discovered. Tanit's image was also used on Carthage's coins. She was associated with doves, palm trees, fish, and pomegranate. These items often accompanied her image. She was also depicted with wings and the head of a lion.

Military

Carthage was engaged in almost constant conflict over territories in the Mediterranean, especially with Greece and Rome. Hannibal Barca entered the Carthaginian world with the backdrop of the First Punic War overshadowing affairs in the Mediterranean city-state, and his father, Hamilcar Barca, was an esteemed general. Over the years, Carthage would use its powerful military to establish new territories in North Africa and places like Corsica and Ibiza. The Carthage military was composed of **mercenary** armies (paid soldiers), their own soldiers, and its impressive navy.

With these components, Carthage became the dominant force in the western Mediterranean from the ninth century BCE until its downfall in the third century BCE. Its accomplished and efficient military allowed Carthage to guard and expand its territories and trading locations throughout the ancient world.

Navy

The jewel of Carthage's military was its immense naval fleet. Carthage warships were incredibly maneuverable and fast, reaching speeds of 7–8 knots (8–9 miles per hour) on manpower alone. Though that may not seem very fast, the ships were larger and faster than anything the ancient world had seen at that time. It was a horrifying sight for enemy ships to see huge Carthaginian quinqueremes barreling down at them. The goal of naval warfare was to destroy the enemy by ramming their vessel, thus causing it to sink. This was a more delicate task than might be expected. Sailors had to be aware of not only speed and movement but also of how hard to hit the enemy so as not to get the battering ram stuck and then be unable to extract it from the cavity it had created. Fleets attempted to ram the enemy in one of two ways. First, they might sail directly towards enemy ships in a straight line, hoping to strike the enemy line head on. The second strategy was to sail down the **flanks** of the enemy fleet's formation and attack from the sides and/or rear. Both attacks were extremely hard to defend against, especially on open water.

Carthage's ships were also used to transport reinforcements and supplies. They attacked enemy supply vessels, acted as escorts for trading ships, and engineered blockades of enemy ports. Carthage was also known to sink the ships of rival traders who were found to be impinging upon Carthaginian trading posts.

DIDO'S CITY

While historians now know that Carthage was founded by Phoenicians who fled Tyre during Alexander the Great's assault on the city, legend has it that Carthage was founded by Queen Elissa of Tyre, referred to in Virgil's the *Aeneid* with the Roman name Dido. As it was told and retold by various authors, the legend varies slightly but tells the tale of Dido's brother Pygmalion swindling her out of her inheritance and killing her husband for profit. Dido flees Tyre, with a group of loyal subjects and some of the king's gold, and sails towards the west looking for a new kingdom. They eventually land on the coast of North Africa where, seeing fertile land, Dido bargains with the inhabitants for a plot. They tell her she can have as much land as she can cover with the hide of an ox. Dido, displaying Carthaginian ingenuity, cut the ox's hide into very thin strips so as to cover a vast expanse of land upon which the kingdom of Carthage was built.

In Virgil's version of Dido's tale, she meets Aeneas, an ancestor of Rome, and falls in love after being shot by Cupid's arrow. The two lovers spend the night in a cave, where Aeneas receives a message from Jupiter telling him to leave her and fulfill his destiny of founding Rome. When Dido awakes to find him gone, she is so distraught that she throws herself into a fire and dies. Before her suicide, she curses Aeneas and all his descendants, foreshadowing the brutal Punic Wars.

Army

Carthage's navy was without a doubt their most powerful military asset. However, in order to compete with enemy forces and continue to claim territories, Carthage had to rely on a land army. Carthage staffed its army with hired mercenaries that hailed from allied territories or areas that Carthage had previously conquered. The Carthage army enjoyed success in Africa, Sicily, Spain, and Italy, led by both Hamilcar and Hannibal Barca. With these successes came the necessity for increased manpower, as more territories meant more conflict with both local tribes and the powers of Greece and Rome.

The citizen army of Carthage included around three thousand infantrymen. They carried white shields and were heavily armored. They lived in barracks within the walls of Carthage. As Carthage was known more for its navy, it relied heavily upon the mercenary soldiers of its allies and conquered territories. These soldiers hailed from places such as Greece, Iberia, Gaul, and Southern Italy. Perhaps the most essential component of these professional soldiers was the Numidian cavalry. These fighters were skilled professionals and carried javelins and small shields. They were also known to use poison darts against enemies

Carthage relied very heavily on these mercenaries and took precautions to ensure that they did not rise up in an attempt to take Carthage for themselves. Mercenaries were commanded by Carthaginian officers at the top and middle levels of office. However, revolt was not always avoidable. After the First Punic War, when Carthage attempted to pay the professional soldiers less, there was an uprising among the mercenaries, which led to Carthage having to deploy their army to **suppress** the same soldiers they had paid to fight alongside them.

CHAPTER TWO

Hannibal's Early Years

As a result of Rome's destruction of Carthage following the Third Punic War, there is little concrete knowledge of Hannibal's childhood. However, we do know that Hannibal's upbringing was most influenced by his father, Hamilcar Barca. Hamilcar was known for his military prowess and strategy but above all, history remembers Hamilcar as a fervent enemy of Rome. After Carthage had surrendered to Rome following the First Punic War, Hamilcar would rebuild his city-state's wealth and military by journeying overseas and introducing his sons to the ways of warfare firsthand.

Born Into Punic War

Hannibal was born into a prestigious military family in the great city of Carthage in the Western Mediterranean. At the time of Hannibal's birth, Rome and Carthage were already bitter rivals engaged in competition for control of the wealthy Mediterranean. In 264 BCE, these two powerful city-states warred over control of the island of Sicily in an effort to dominate the region. The

Opposite: This relief sculpture marks the grave of a Carthaginian child, one of few remaining artifacts from Hannibal's home.

First Punic War was fought primarily at sea by way of massive naval battles along Sicily's coast. For twenty-three years, both sides battled fiercely without either opponent gaining much advantage. Finally Rome edged Carthage out and was able to take control of Sicily, though much of Carthage's military campaign had been successful. His father, Hamilcar, had gone unbeaten throughout the war. In fact, Hamilcar was so successful in his campaigns throughout Sicily and the Italian coastline that he earned the nickname "Barca" which meant "Thunderbolt." His descendants also adopted Barca as a surname, identifying themselves with the great general. The events and aftermath of the First Punic War would shape Hannibal's generation and come to define his life's purpose under his father's influence.

Aftermath of the First Punic War

The Romans used their victory as an opportunity to reduce the power of their rivals and impose harsh penalties upon Carthage. Under the conditions of surrender, they demanded an **indemnity** paid to Rome, a withdrawal of all Carthaginian claims to Sicily, and the almost complete dismantling of Carthage's robust navy. Carthaginians were outraged by the **punitive** terms issued by an enemy who only barely defeated them. The Roman attitude of superiority was almost too much for the proud Carthaginians to bear.

One Carthage veteran would struggle especially hard to accept Roman defeat. Hannibal's father, Hamilcar Barca, returned from the first Punic War heavy-hearted and stunned at Carthage's surrender. A Carthaginian general, he had experienced his very first loss to Rome in his military career, not of his own doing but as a result of decisions made by the Carthage senate. Hamilcar was exceptionally bitter about the loss because he had seen only victories in battle and thought that the Carthaginian government had given in to Rome too easily. With a longing for revenge against the Romans, Hamilcar reentered domestic life among his family. His son Hannibal was six years old.

As if the recent surrender to their most dangerous rival and the crushing terms that they were dealt were not enough problems for Carthage, the city-state soon faced a mutiny at the hands of their own army. Carthage was unlike other city-states in that their army was not composed completely of their own citizens. The Carthage army was made up of people from across the Mediterranean who were hired as paid mercenaries to fight on behalf of Carthage. Hamilcar had commanded a force of 20,000 of these soldiers over the course of the first Punic War and in 241 BCE sent them back to North Africa with the promise of receiving payment for their efforts in the near future. Carthage then sent less money than they had originally promised, angering the hired soldiers and leading them to revolt. Hamilcar was called back to battle to suppress the mutiny. The job of defeating the very men he used to command did not seem to bother Hamilcar in the least. In fact, he seemed to relish the punishment of his former troops, engaging in ruthless punishment of the mutinous. He would either kill the soldiers with his blade or tie them up and have them trampled beneath his massive elephants.

Still Threatened by Rome

While Hamilcar was busy with trying to quell rebellion, Rome was seizing even more land in the western Mediterranean. In 238 BCE, Roman forces took control of the islands of Corsica and Sardinia, areas that had been Carthaginian strongholds for centuries. The Romans claimed that Carthage had assaulted merchants who were traveling from Rome to Sardinia and that this justified their appropriation of the islands. Romans valued the idea that they only engaged in war when an opponent had openly attacked them or swore allegiance to Rome. This self-righteousness often led them to make **dubious** claims regarding such attacks.

Hamilcar was **incensed**. With Carthage's economic and military power waning as a result of Roman dictates, he knew he would have to travel elsewhere to rebuild Carthage's martial and monetary prowess. Carthage looked west to Iberia, what is now Spain. Spain offered the resources the Carthaginians would need in order to recover their glory, including gold and silver mines as well as proven soldiers. Carthage had colonies in Spain, and Hamilcar hoped to recruit manpower as well as establish a military base in the region. Legend has it that nine-year-old Hannibal begged to be allowed to accompany his father and the troops on their voyage. The night before the trip, Hamilcar prepared to make a human sacrifice in the hopes of a successful journey. He led young Hannibal to the altar and had the boy rest his hand on the victim and swear that he would be an enemy of Rome forever.

Recruitment in Spain

Once in Spain, Hamilcar and his men set out to build alliances with local chiefs in an effort to persuade them to contribute men to the Carthaginian army. If diplomacy failed, military force was swiftly meted out. The Greek historian Polybius estimates that Hamilcar spent nearly nine years in Spain recruiting tribes through negotiation or dominance. All the while, Hannibal and his two brothers, Mago and Hasdrubal, watched their father exert his will on Spain. The growing army took a liking to the three boys and referred to them as the Lion's Brood. The boys were raised far from their native land among traveling warriors for the express purpose of becoming skilled soldiers themselves. They ate, slept, played, and trained with the diverse fighters, all the while listening to their father's tales of vengeance they would enact upon the Romans.

In 229 BCE, the roaming army laid siege to the city of Helice. A local Spanish chieftain approached with troops under the guise of being in alliance with the Carthaginians. At an opportune moment, the newcomers ambushed the army. Not wanting to put his boys in danger, Hamilcar drew his attackers away from his sons and found himself caught between his rapidly advancing attackers and a raging river. Seeing he had little chance of escape, Hamilcar rode his horse into the rapids and died. His son-in-law, Hasdrubal the Fair, took up command of the diverse military until his own death, at which point the soldiers looked to their second in command, young Hannibal, to lead them.

After his father's death, Hannibal was named supreme military commander of Carthage at the age of twenty-six. The soldiers had watched Hannibal grow from a boy to an effective soldier whose leadership and verve in battle inspired comparisons with his father. He lived and fought among the men, and they enthusiastically proclaimed his commanding position to the Carthaginian powers back home. Carthage had no choice but to accept the unanimously lauded young general.

A General's Childhood

Modern-day historians know very little about Hannibal Barca's childhood. The oath Hannibal is said to have taken against Rome is consistently mentioned by ancient historians, but outside of this oft-told tale, the young Hannibal's life is a mystery. Hannibal's mother is also a mystery, though it is believed that she may have been from another country, as it was common practice for Carthage men to take foreign wives. It is known that Hannibal spent his childhood in military camps in modern-day Spain and learned hand-to-hand combat from the hardened soldiers who fought under his father's leadership. In fact, Hannibal's father was arguably his most important teacher and mentor in terms of military prowess. Hannibal's education was decidedly hands-on, as he watched his father's army fight and conquer. This education would have been hard for young Hannibal to digest, as military leaders who failed in battle were often publicly crucified.

Hannibal is said to have married an Iberian woman named Imilce from the town of Castulo, before taking command of the army and setting off in pursuit of conflict with Rome. While Hannibal is reported to have taken control of Carthage forces at age twenty-six, historians are uncertain as to how old Hannibal may have been at the time of his wedding. While it is possible that the two had children, there are no records indicating that his offspring survived if they existed at all.

A Military Education

Hannibal spent his early years under the tutelage of military men, including his father and those that served under him. Along with his two brothers, Hannibal was schooled in the art of war firsthand. Being brought up in military camp would have meant learning to ride and fight on horseback as well as lessons in strategy and military command. Being that Hamilcar Barca was a prestigious general and a member of an elite Carthage clan, the boys would have been taught academic subjects by tutors. Historian Cornelius Nepos tells us that a Spartan named Sosylus

Hannibal was schooled in Greek traditions, which would have included language, politics, philosophy and of course wrestling.

was responsible for teaching Hannibal Greek. Sosylus passed down lessons in Greek language, politics, and leadership.

Belief in Melqart

Hannibal was a devotee of the Phoenician and Carthaginian god, Melqart. The Roman historian Livy writes that prior to his march towards Italy, Hannibal journeyed to Gades, an ancient site of Phoenician worship. He is said to have prayed and sacrificed at the Altar of Melqart before returning to Spain to prepare for the voyage. The night before the army was set to depart, Hannibal received a vision he believed to have been sent from the god himself.

A beautiful youth appeared to the general that night and said that he had been sent by Melqart to shepherd the son of Hamilcar to Italy. The vision spoke to Hannibal, "Follow me and see that thou look not behind thee." Hannibal followed the ghostly vision

This image illustrates the Festival of Melqart celebrated in ancient Carthage; this revered god also inspired Hannibal.

but eventually succumbed to temptation and glanced backwards. Hannibal saw a giant snake thrashing through a forest, destroying everything in its path. It moved like an ominous storm, and thunder boomed and lightning flashed in its wake. Hannibal asked his visitor what he was seeing, to which he replied, "What thou beholdest is the desolation of Italy. Follow thy star and inquire no farther into the dark counsels of heaven." Upon waking, Hannibal shared the vision with his men, and bolstered with new confidence, the army set out to test their fate.

Hannibal's Physical Appearance

There has been much debate and speculation among scholars regarding Hannibal's physical appearance, especially surrounding his ethnicity. We have no description of his physicality that has survived to modern age. The most we know about Hannibal's looks from description is that he may have disguised himself at times. It is impossible to know whether minted coins from Spain that might bear his image are of Hannibal, his father Hamilcar, or another Carthaginian associated with the campaign in Spain. Matters are further complicated when considering that Rome likely recalled any coinage bearing his likeness when Carthage was destroyed. These coins were probably melted down and recast with images of Roman aristocracy. Apart from artifacts, we have no DNA evidence to make conjecture regarding Hannibal's physicality. There are no skeletal fragments, hair follicles, etc. All we have as a map to guide us towards what Hannibal might have looked like is what we know of his family ancestry. Hannibal is believed to be descended from Phoenician aristocracy. Even this we cannot be completely sure of because so many different people moved into the region at the time of Hannibal's life and certainly

This bust of Hannibal was created by the Spanish sculptor Juan José Quirós.

since his death. If it is true, then Hannibal and his ancestors would have come from what is now Lebanon. Unfortunately, all of this is speculative. It is impossible to know what Hannibal may have looked like in terms of ethnicity as he lived more than two thousand years ago and DNA has changed quite a bit since then.

While there isn't enough evidence to make a confident distinction in terms of Hannibal's race, it is safe to assume that Hannibal was athletic in appearance. Having spent his life marching and waging war, he probably had the physique of a battle-worn soldier. We do know that he lost sight in one of his eyes while pursuing the Romans and may have worn an eye patch of sorts in his later days.

Family Influences

Hannibal spent his life waging military campaigns in foreign lands, but his kin traveled either alongside him or in pursuit of common goals throughout his life. From his father, he inherited his life's mission of wreaking havoc upon Rome and also his strategy in battle and conquest. Hannibal's two brothers, Mago and Hasdrubal, served in the army he commanded and had a similar passion for bringing death to the Romans. Though Hannibal kept Carthage close to his heart, he spent most of his life far from his beloved city. From the time he was nine years old until around the age of forty-five, he roamed the Mediterranean with only his soldiers, his brothers, and his father as immediate influences.

Hamilcar Barca

Hamilcar Barca, Hannibal's father, was arguably the most influential person in Hannibal's life. After all, Hannibal received his life's mission of battling Rome forever from Hamilcar. He also learned to fight, strategize, and recruit soldiers from his father's example. Hannibal was Hamilcar's firstborn son and thus the burden of his father's expectations probably fell heaviest on Hannibal of all his children. Nothing is known of Hamilcar before 247 BCE, when he took command of Carthaginian forces in Sicily during the second Punic War. Though he was able to launch impressive guerrilla attacks on the Romans occupying the island, Carthage was defeated by the Romans at sea, and a peace treaty was signed with Rome, much to Hamilcar's shock and dismay. After the war drew to a close, Hamilcar had to fight the very mercenaries that he had led against Rome. It is not unreasonable to think that these events may have led Hamilcar to pass down not only hatred of Rome to his sons, but distrust of the Carthaginian senate and the necessity of monitoring and subduing mercenary forces. Battling alongside his sons in modern day Spain would have taught young Hannibal to model his father's diplomacy tactics of leading with charisma and persuasion, and if those didn't work, then using force to sway local tribes to ally themselves with Carthage. Hannibal used these same strategies when engaging the Italians after crossing the Alps, albeit without as much success as he'd hoped and needed. The similarities between Hannibal and his father were recognized by the soldiers Hamilcar led. In fact, after the murder of Hasdrubal the Fair, Hamilcar's son-in-law who took command of the troops in the aftermath of his suicide, the troops resoundingly selected Hannibal to be their new leader. It is believed that Hamilcar's likeness, as seen in his son, was inspiring to the soldiers. Hamilcar's influence on Hannibal can be found even in death. Hamilcar chose to throw himself into the rapids of the Jucar River rather than be caught and killed by enraged tribes that pursued him. Hannibal chose to die a similar death, opting for suicide by poison when it became clear that he had been betrayed by the King of Prussia and capture by the Romans was imminent as a result. Artists and scholars remain fascinated by the curious relationship between this father and son.

Brothers in Arms

Along with Hannibal's father, his brothers accompanied him in his military training and education as well as his campaign against Rome. Though they did not always fight alongside Hannibal, they were instrumental in his assaults during the Second Punic War. Mago, the youngest of the three boys, participated in the invasion of Italy and commanded troops during the first three years of the Second Punic War. After the Battle of Cannae, he was sent to Spain to join Hasdrubal, Hamilcar's second-oldest son, in the fight against the Roman **consuls** Publius Cornelius Scipio and Gnaeus Cornelius Scipio. They were successful in killing the Roman leaders but did not see the same success in fighting Publius's son, who would later defeat Hannibal and be renamed Scipio Africanus. Mago would take his fight to Italy, where he would die in 203 BCE. In 207 BCE, Hasdrubal was able to make his own crossing of the Alps in order to fight the Romans in Italy. Though he traversed the Alps, he would die in battle shortly thereafter. The Romans were said to have decapitated his corpse and then transported it to Hannibal's camp, where they threw the head of his younger brother into Hannibal's base as a sign of impending defeat.

Through the Ages

Hannibal's legacy has been passed down through history by those who feared him and had been defeated by him in battle. Though the Romans eventually conquered Carthage, they despised the city-state and Hannibal as well. In fact, the term Punic is derived from a Roman slur referencing the Phoenicians. History reflects Rome's domination of the ancient world, especially but not predictably in terms of Hannibal Barca. The two historians who are most referenced by modern scholars are the Greek historian Polybius and the Roman historian Titus Livius, better known as Livy. Though both scholars document the efforts of Hannibal, their methods and focus deviate from each other as they chose to highlight different aspects of the events of Hannibal's life.

Greek Historian Polybius

The historian who lived closest to Hannibal's time and arguably provides the most objective account relied upon by modern scholars is Polybius. Though Polybius was Greek, his writings detail Rome's rise to power. Polybius is unique in that he had personal connections with those who had engaged Hannibal in battle, thus his recordings went beyond mere conjecture and recitation of prior authors. Polybius had some military knowledge because he had been a cavalry general, but his life changed when he was taken prisoner by Rome around 167 BCE. Approximately one thousand Greeks were taken political prisoner for not taking Rome's side in its war against Macedonia. Polybius was ordered by Aemilius Paulus to educate his children, Fabius and Scipio, who had been adopted by Scipio Africanus, the general who defeated Hannibal. Scipio and Polybius grew and remained close. Scipio, and his ties to those who knew and fought with and against Hannibal, was a great resource for Polybius while he wrote his *Histories*, which spans 118 years from 264 BCE to 146 BCE. As a historian, Polybius believed that it was his duty to remain objective. He criticized other historians who had come before him for revealing their biases in their recording of events. Polybius writes:

This statue of Polybius sits outside the Parliament building in Vienna, Austria.

... the peculiar function of history is to discover, in the first place, the words actually spoken, whatever they were, and next to ascertain the reason why what was done or spoken led to failure or success. For the mere statement of fact may interest us but is of no benefit to us: but when we add the cause of it, study of history becomes fruitful.

PRESENTING HANNIBAL

Dr. Eve MacDonald is a modern historian and archaeologist who has studied Hannibal and the Punic Wars in detail. Dr. MacDonald has taken part in excavations in a variety of locales including the Middle East, the ruins of ancient Carthage, and various settings throughout the Mediterranean. Her recent work, *Hannibal: A Hellenistic Life*, considers Hannibal in the context of the changing society he was surrounded by. While his exploits and military prowess are examined in this well-rounded text, so too is Carthage's rise to power and descent under Roman provocation. Dr. MacDonald has taught in a number of higher educational institutions across the UK and Canada and is currently serving as a sessional lecturer in the Department of Classics at the University of Reading in England. While Dr. MacDonald is most engaged in writing about the life and times of Hannibal, in May of 2015 she took some time out of her schedule to imagine what a movie of her book might look like for the blog "My Book, The Movie." Here is how she fantasized *Hannibal: A Hellenistic Life* would be portrayed:

> A sword and sandals epic comes to mind—part *Gladiator*, part *Alexander the Great*—but there was no happy ending to Hannibal's story, no redemption for him or Carthage … I have often thought about who should play Hannibal in a film; it would have to be an actor who could convey the right mix of brave soldier and wise, charismatic and inspirational leader … Javier Bardem would be perfect because I think he could convey the complexity of Hannibal's character, a man with razor sharp intelligence and a hugely inspirational leader…"

Polybius is also known for asserting, "If history is deprived of the Truth, we are left with nothing but an idle unprofitable tale." With his fondness for accuracy evident, he also writes glowingly of Hannibal and his exploits. This could be due to his own bias in his newfound love for Rome or simply because Hannibal was truly masterful. In either case Polybius references Hannibal as "an extraordinary product of nature." He goes on to say that "no one can withhold admiration for Hannibal's generalship, courage, and power in the field."

Roman Historian Livy

Another primary source that historians rely on in order to concoct a picture of Hannibal is the work of the Roman historian Titus Livius, or Livy. Not much is known about Livy or his family. Scholars do know that his recording of history was motivated by a fascination with the character of man and how character determines actions and thus history itself. He was less interested in scholarly accuracy and more focused on reconstructing the work of historians who had come before him and bringing out the moral standards of those involved in order to make the work relevant to his contemporaries.

His **seminal** work, *History of Rome*, offers one of our only detailed accounts of Hannibal's exploits. However, because of Livy's Roman heritage, his words must be read with the understanding that his opinion was probably skewed by Roman feelings about the Carthaginian general who truly threatened the existence of the republic during his command of the Carthage army. Livy's account of Hannibal's personal habits is one of self-sacrifice and denial. Livy writes:

This engraving depicts the Roman historian Livy whose most famous work is *The History of Rome*, which details the empire's ascent to power.

No toil could exhaust his body or overcome his spirit. He could endure heat and cold alike, and his consumption of food and

> drink was determined by natural want and not by pleasure. His times of sleeping and waking were not determined by night or day. Once his work was done he gave what time remained to rest, but he did not court this with a soft bed or quiet. Many have often seen him lying on the ground wrapped only in a military coat amid the sentries and outposts of his soldiers.

Here we see an image of Hannibal as almost superhuman, enduring extreme temperatures and eating and drinking not for pleasure but strictly for necessity. He goes on little sleep, and the sleep he does get occurs on the ground with his soldiers. Some of this must be true given his daring exploits, especially during the winter months. However, historians are conscious of the Roman hand that wrote these and other words about Hannibal and debate the character and habits of a man who is long gone and of whom little is known.

When Hannibal first appears in Livy's work, it is Hasdrubal who is in command of the Carthaginian forces with Hannibal serving as a captain. Livy details how awestruck the soldiers are to see the young Hannibal after the death of his father.

> The older soldiers thought that a young Hamilcar had been brought back to them; they saw that same dynamism in his expression, the same forcefulness in his eyes, the same facial expressions and features . . .

With these passages, Livy situates the narrative of Hannibal as a son doing his duty as passed down by his father, to the point that he almost becomes his father. These words underline Hamilcar's influence on Hannibal and make the bond between father and son mythic in nature.

CHAPTER THREE

Hannibal *versus* Rome

While Hannibal's father was an acclaimed general in the Carthage army, his son would go on to become one of the most brave, innovative, and effective military leaders in the history of the world. As a result of his childhood spent traveling across Spain with his father and the Carthaginian army, Hannibal was steeped in the ways of combat. He and his two brothers had watched his father successfully galvanize multinational forces to a common goal and bonded with the soldiers as they grew into men. After his father's suicide and the assassination of Hasdrubal The Fair, his father's successor, Hannibal was selected to head the conglomerate fighting force.

Preparing to Fight

The Carthaginians didn't just travel to Spain in order to recruit manpower for their army. As the soldiers marched across Spain, they established territories in the name of Carthage. One of these towns was New Carthage. Located on the eastern coast of Spain, New Carthage served as a vital military base. Its expansive bay

Opposite: Hannibal loved incorporating his massive, awe-inspiring African elephants in his military campaigns.

could accommodate many ships, while the bay's narrow entrance allowed for easy patrol. Not only was the location of New Carthage optimal for naval deployment, the military outpost also had access to considerable wealth. Mines situated to the east of New Carthage produced a mass of silver and lead, which allowed the Carthaginians to begin to accumulate new riches. This new wealth helped the Carthaginians to continue to pay indemnity to Rome as a condition of the end of the First Punic War. Thousands more soldiers were recruited as New Carthage gained power. Minted coins were produced featuring portraits of soldiers. Spain's wealth of manpower and economic resources allowed Carthage to not only raise an army but also provide supplies and feed the recruits. With all of its assets, its location was probably the most attractive to the revenge-focused Hannibal. New Carthage was in close proximity to Italy, providing easy access to Rome.

Treaty of River Ebro

In the third century BCE, as Carthage marched across Spain amassing wealth and manpower, Rome grew more and more anxious about their rival's exploits. Hannibal and his army pushed their way up through northern Spain, prompting Rome to send representatives to Spain in order to negotiate a treaty with Carthage. The agreement would attempt to stop Carthaginians from moving any further north by using the River Ebro as a boundary. The Romans agreed not to travel south of Ebro, and in turn, Carthage would acknowledge the river as its northernmost limit in Spain. Carthage agreed to the treaty. Hannibal continued to seize Spanish territories in the name of Carthage, but he and his men did not travel beyond the agreed-upon boundary. However, that would not be the end of Rome's interference.

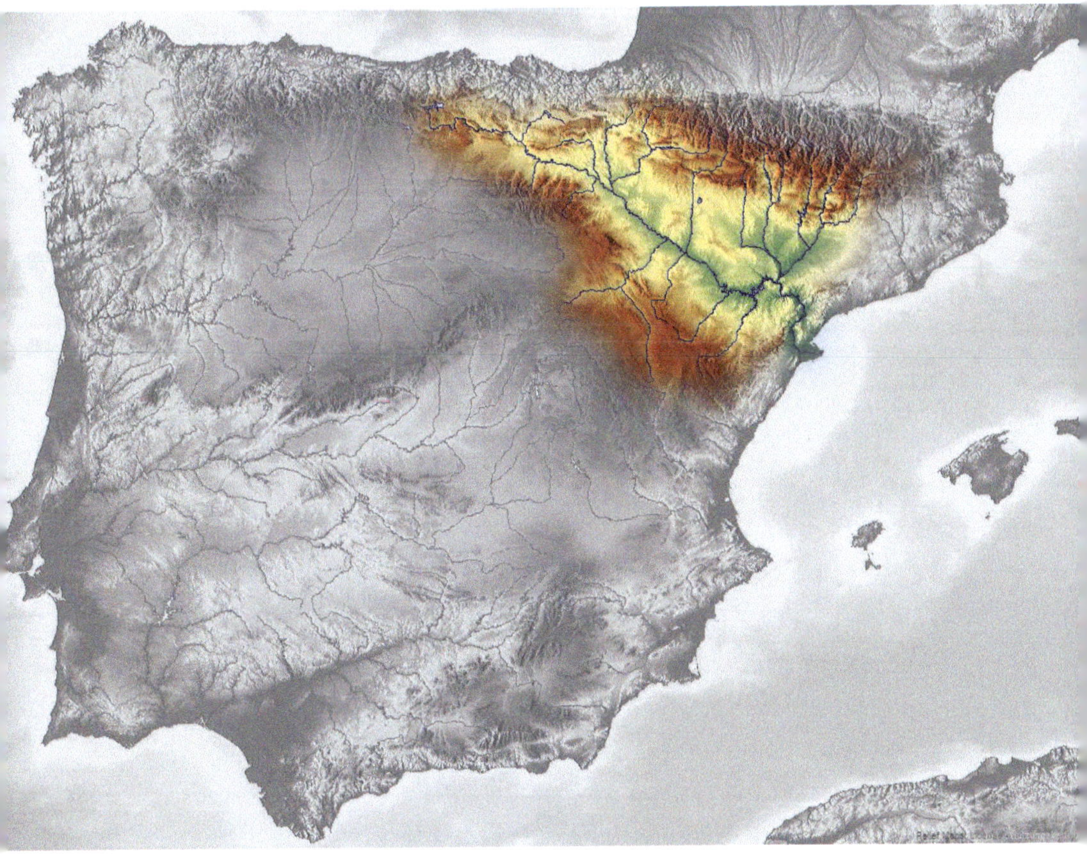

The highlighted portion of this map is the River Ebro. Rome agreed not to move south of this boundary but continued to meddle in the region.

In 220 BCE, Roman ambassadors traveled to Spain with further conditions for the Carthaginians. They warned Hannibal against attacking the city of Saguntum, located just south of the River Ebro. The emissaries claimed that the citizens of Saguntum had sworn alliance to Rome. In typical Roman fashion, they set up conditions for war under the thinly veiled guise of diplomacy. Hannibal responded by attacking Saguntum. While he laid siege to Saguntum, the Romans sent out a delegation to the city telling Hannibal to cease his attack. Hannibal refused, and the delegation headed to Carthage. The Romans delivered an ultimatum upon arrival. Carthage could either denounce Hannibal's actions, arrest the general and deliver him to Rome, or face another war with their fiercest rival. The leader of the Roman embassy is said to have spoken the words, "In the fold of my toga, I can give you either peace or war." The Carthaginians chose war. Hannibal had managed to initiate conflict with the Romans, giving him an opportunity to fulfill his father's dream of serving revenge to Carthage's former conqueror.

Different Armies

While Carthage had managed to regain much of its strength and wealth in the two decades since defeat in the First Punic War, their power was dwarfed by the empire Rome had become. With all of the western Mediterranean now under Rome's command, the burgeoning superpower had unmatched access to fresh recruits. The Greek historian Polybius tells us that Rome's manpower was estimated to be over 700,000 adult men. The Roman army's structure and strategy also differed from the Carthaginian force.

In order to take full advantage of their massive military, Rome would split their soldiers into two separate armies. The Romans held annual elections to determine who would lead each faction. These consuls would serve as co-presidents of the Roman state during their term. The balance of power was very important to Roman politics, so the consuls were required to engage in unanimous decision making. In 218 BCE, Rome elected Publius Cornelius Scipio and Tybius Sinpronius Longus as consuls.

Together, they determined a strategy. One army would confront Hannibal in Saguntum, while the other army would make its way through Sicily and on to North Africa in order to lay waste to Carthage and take revenge on the Carthaginian senate that had refused to condemn and deliver Hannibal.

While the Romans had a wealth of soldiers, their military was composed of largely untested citizens. Carthage, on the other hand, had an army of one hundred thousand dedicated, loyal, professional soldiers who adored their charismatic leader and spent their lives fighting together. Hannibal's army was incredibly diverse, with soldiers from across the Mediterranean. They fought with different weapons and armor, but all followed Hannibal without incidence of mutiny. The Numidian cavalry, for example, was one of the deadliest units in ancient warfare and consistently flanked Hannibal's infantry. They served as scouts and as a corralling force in battle against the Romans. As the soldiers won victories against Rome, they took armor and weapons from the dead. This upgrade in equipment made them even more effective.

Not only did Hannibal have veteran soldiers, he also had a team of Carthage engineers among his fighting force. Rome's soldiers were amateur in comparison. In addition to his highly trained army, Hannibal also had a massive **war chest** and thirty-seven African elephants. Inspired by Alexander the Great, Carthage were fond of using elephants in battle. These enormous animals were terrifying to infantrymen and cavalry soldiers alike. Fighting an enemy who rode into battle with elephants was incredibly disorienting. Not only were the beasts huge, their loud noises and giant tusks frightened many opposing soldiers, some of whom had never even seen an elephant. Some armies would flee on sight of these intimidating creatures. However, Hannibal knew

This map shows Hannibal's route of attack during the Second Punic War.

he would need more than a few dozen elephants to defeat Rome.

Hannibal recognized that he would have to be proactive and strike Rome where it would hurt most: on their own soil. In order to do this, he would have to figure out how to get his army from Spain to Italy in order to encroach upon Rome. Invading by sea was not an option because of Carthage's reduced naval resources. Hannibal developed a plan that would be marveled at by military strategists for centuries to come. He would lead his men on an extended march through the French Alps, straight to Rome's doorstep.

Crossing of the Alps

In the spring of 218 BCE, Hannibal and his army made their way towards Italy with a thousand miles of treacherous rivers and mountain ranges in their path. At the same time, Scipio and his men moved towards Spain, while Longus headed to Sicily. While Scipio camped in France, he received word that Hannibal and his army had entered southern France. Scipio readied himself for battle, thinking that Hannibal was planning on attacking. Hannibal instead continued north towards Italy, bypassing Scipio completely.

At the foot of the French Alps, Hannibal and his engineers faced their first major challenge on the banks of the Rhône River. The task of transporting the entire army, 12,000 horses and 37 elephants across the rolling river, which was anywhere from 330 to 650 feet (100 to 198 m) wide, would demand incredible innovation. Not only did the Carthage army need to figure out how to cross the Rhône, they also faced hostile tribes spoiling for battle on the opposite shore. Hannibal's soldiers quickly began gathering large conifers from the nearby forest and binding the massive trees with rope to create a series of large rafts. Each raft was around 200 feet (61 m) long and 50 feet (15 m) wide. Hannibal's engineers even accounted for the mindset of the elephants. The sides of the giant rafts were piled with layers of sticks and soil to obscure the elephants' vision. In this way, the Carthaginians hoped to prevent the gargantuan animals from becoming frightened and potentially causing the rafts to capsize. Once assembled, the vessels were loaded with animals, supplies, and soldiers. They floated en masse toward the opposite shore. The hostile natives who had been waiting for the Carthaginians fled at the sight of the mammoth operation floating towards them. Not only was the undertaking ingenious and successful, it took Hannibal and his men a total of only nine days to plan and execute.

Hannibal's army reached the foot of the French Alps in November; they would be making their crossing in the heart of a freezing mountain winter. It is said that Hannibal's men stood awestruck and frightened as the reality of their task set in. To rouse them Hannibal made an impassioned speech:

> Year after year you have fought with me and won. When finally you have the Alps in sight and know that the other side of them is Italian soil, you come to a halt, exhausted. Either confess then that you have less spirit and courage than a people you have again and again defeated during these latter days or steal your hearts to march forward, to halt only on Mars' field between the Tiber and the walls of Rome.

With a newly inspired fighting force, Hannibal made the trek through two weeks of unforgiving snowstorms, attacks from unwelcoming natives, and hazardous temperatures. Historians have marveled at the Carthaginians' intrepid task of traversing the mountain ranges along with thirty-seven immense African elephants and thousands of horses. While some parts of the mountain could be scaled, massive sections of rock made it impossible for the soldiers to ascend with their animals in tow. One theory about how this was accomplished involves both climbing and destroying parts of the mountain. The Roman historian Livy explains that Hannibal and his team of engineers surmounted this obstacle by cutting large gaps into the boulders and then laying wood gathered from the forest at the base of the cracked rocks and lighting a fire. As the fire burned, the temperature of the rocks rose. Hannibal's engineers would then pour boiling vinegar over the heated rocks, causing them to either crack further or melt depending on how hot they had become.

Freezing temperatures and treacherous terrain were not the only obstacles that Hannibal and his men had to overcome. Over the two weeks they spent traversing the Alps, they were attacked multiple times by hostile tribes. On one occasion, they were lured into a narrow pass and ambushed from above as the tribe hailed large boulders upon the soldiers as they attempted to make their way through the tapered road. As the army climbed higher and higher, more and more soldiers succumbed to death. Some sources report that Hannibal lost as many as fifty thousand men while traveling from Spain to Italy. Despite these losses, the remaining army and animals made their way out of the Alps and reached the Po Valley. After four months spent traveling through Spain and fifteen days in the French Alps, the Carthaginian army reached the Po Valley in Northern Italy. The residents of the valley were stunned at the sight of Hannibal's army and their herd of elephants looking down on them from the hills above. Word of Hannibal's successful journey into Italy reached Scipio shortly thereafter. The Roman consul was forced to face the fact that he had gravely underestimated his enemy, and as a result, Rome faced an imminent, legitimate threat.

The Battle of Ticinus

While Hannibal was relentless in his pursuit of Rome, he had lost tens of thousands of men and several elephants in the preceding months. His army was depleted and exhausted, but the Po Valley offered an abundance of resources. With its ample grain, lush vineyards, and plenty of livestock, Hannibal was able to replenish supplies and rejuvenate his men while they rested. At the same time, Hannibal knew he would have to focus his efforts on obtaining fresh soldiers.

Hannibal would have to depend on the Gauls living in Italy to provide soldiers. He once again made contacts with local tribes with the purpose of recruiting troops. The Gauls were a fierce people who excelled at hand-to-hand combat and favored the use of a double-edged sword in battle. The Romans had defeated them less than ten years prior to Hannibal's arrival. They hated the Romans, and many enthusiastically joined the Carthage effort to wreak havoc on their mutual conqueror. There was some resistance to Hannibal's recruitment effort. The Turini tribes, in modern day Turin, were angry about Carthaginian soldiers traipsing across Italy. Hannibal responded by laying siege to Turin and murdering the resistant tribe members. Others who may have been inclined to resist enlisting were convinced by the brutality of Hannibal's response. Hannibal's ranks continued to swell.

As the Gauls began to join Hannibal in his mission, Rome was forced to face the reality that two of the republic's greatest enemies were allied in their desire for revenge. As Hannibal's growing army marched through Spain, Scipio marched through the Po Valley, forcing remaining Gauls to join the Roman army.

By December of 218 BCE, Hannibal had recruited twenty thousand men, leaving him with approximately forty-six thousand soldiers in total. They marched west along the Po River while Scipio marched eastward to meet them at the Ticinus River. On the cusp of battle with Scipio, Hannibal once again roused his men.

> There is not one of you that has not with his own eyes seen me strike a blow in battle. I have watched and witnessed your valor in the field and your acts of courage I know by heart. I was your

pupil before I was your commander. You must be brave. For you there is no middle way between victory and death. Should fortune hesitate to favor you, meet death in battle rather than in flight. God has given man no sharper spur to victory than contempt of death.

Both armies led their attack with cavalry units, leaving the bulk of the army to enter the battlefield in their wake. Hannibal sent six thousand cavalrymen, and Scipio sent cavalry as well as a light infantry unit armed with javelins. Scipio formed his cavalry into two lines, with the **velites** in the first and the cavalry units following behind. Hannibal's cavalry was formed into a single line with three sections. His heavy cavalry, including soldiers riding in on elephants, was positioned in the center while two flanking units were positioned on opposite sides. As Hannibal's cavalry rushed into battle at full speed, the velites were overwhelmed and quickly fled back to the second Roman line. A chaotic clash ensued, and the fighting was at a stalemate for a long while. Eventually Hannibal's flanking cavalry were able to cut around the Roman cavalry, trample the retreating velites, and attack the remaining Romans from behind, effectively pinning the Romans between themselves and the heavy cavalry units of the Carthaginian army. The Romans fled, and even Scipio was seriously wounded. His son was among his soldiers and was able to help Scipio escape the fighting.

Polybius explains that this victory was crucial to Hannibal's cause because it bolstered his new recruits; many local chieftains renewed their allegiance to Carthage in the aftermath. Scipio's army experienced a revolt as he fled from battle. The Gauls, whom he had pressured into Roman service, rose up and killed Roman soldiers, decapitating some of the bodies. As the Gauls then made their way to join Hannibal, Scipio moved west to Trebbia, ending the first major battle of the Second Punic War.

The Battle of Trebbia

After Hannibal's victory at Ticinus, he proceeded to seize Roman territories, confiscating grain and taking prisoners. He took mercy upon his prisoners and did not cause them unnecessary harm. His continued recruitment of new soldiers was a prerequisite to success against Rome, and he knew that he would need to appeal to local populations in order to gain manpower. Murdering prisoners would not serve his interests. Hannibal was no saint, and his army would **raze** a town periodically, but this generally occurred after all other efforts at persuasion had been exhausted.

With Scipio wounded, Simpronius Longus was the sole consul still able to fight against Carthage. As the end of his tenure rapidly approached, he was anxious to secure a decisive victory against Hannibal, thus allowing him to taste the glory of a Roman victory celebration before a new consul was elected. Hannibal was excited to enter battle because he knew another victory would aid his recruitment efforts. He also wanted to defeat Longus while Scipio recovered from his wounds, thereby crippling the leadership of the Roman army.

As the two armies approached each other on the Trebbia River, Hannibal spotted a marshy drainage ditch where it would be possible to conceal a significant number of soldiers for ambush during battle. He selected two thousand of his troops, commanded by his brother Mago, to hide in the marsh and wait for an opportune time to strike. Hannibal planned to lure the Roman army forward, positioning them so that the drainage ditch concealing his ambush was behind their front line. He enacted his plan by deploying cavalry soldiers early in the morning to engage in hit-and-run attacks against the Romans while the bulk of his army awoke and ate breakfast.

Hannibal's cavalry would repeatedly strike the Romans and then draw back, spurring Rome to go on the attack under the impression that the cavalry was retreating in fear. The unfed Romans pursued Hannibal's cavalry across the freezing Trebbia River, leaving them exhausted. In contrast, Hannibal's army was well rested and had been fed by the time the Romans were within fighting range. Once Simpronius's army crossed the Trebbia, Hannibal placed his army in formation. Again, Hannibal planned to outflank the Romans. As the light infantry of both armies clashed, Hannibal ordered his flanking cavalry to charge, and they were successful in reaching the second line of Roman soldiers. As Rome's flanks collapsed, Hannibal's hidden forces, now perfectly positioned behind Roman lines, sprang up from the marsh and ambushed the unsuspecting enemy. This created mass confusion. Many of the soldiers fled towards the Trebbia and were either slaughtered or drowned. The Romans were able to inflict great losses on the center of Hannibal's line, and Hannibal lost many elephants as a result of both combat and the freezing temperatures. Nonetheless, Hannibal's military strategizing proved to be superior, as he was able to lure the Romans into a perfectly placed trap. Simpronius Longus ended his term as consul having lost two-thirds of the Roman army, and Hannibal secured another victory against Rome.

The Battle of Lake Trasimene

Hannibal had seen victory in two battles against Rome and had captured or killed tens of thousands of Roman soldiers.

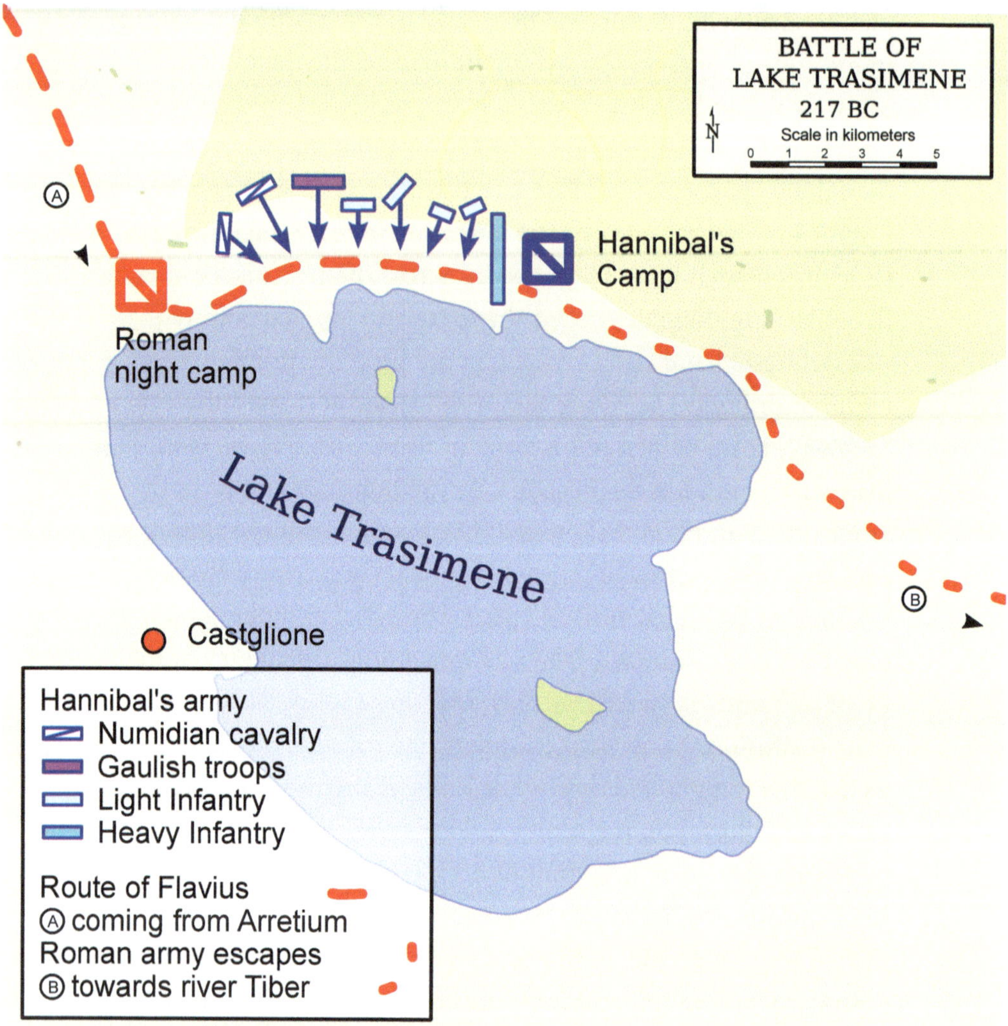

Well-planned battle formations at Lake Trasimene allowed Hannibal the element of surprise against Roman forces.

However, the Gauls began to lose interest in continuing the battle on their soil. Hannibal and his army marched south through Etruria by way of swampy marshlands that allowed them to move undetected by the Romans. Hannibal placed his veteran soldiers at the front, the Gauls followed the veterans, and his brother Mago and the cavalry brought up the rear. Hannibal was concerned about the Gauls defecting, and Mago was given orders to use cavalry forces to compel the Gauls to continue the journey should they try to break formation. The journey was long and **arduous**. All but one elephant died, and Hannibal contracted an infection which caused him to lose sight in one eye. Despite the hardships, they made their way to Arretium, just north of the Tiber River and Rome, where a new Roman consul and his army were camped.

Since Simpronius Longus's failure at the Battle of Trebbia, Rome elected two new consuls, Gaius Flaminius Nepos and Gnaeus Servilius Geminus. Prior to Hannibal's march, Flaminius had positioned himself at Arretium while Servilius was stationed to the northwest at Arminium. Once Hannibal arrived outside Arretium, he knew he had the element of surprise on his side. The Romans were shocked at his presence, and Hannibal wanted to attack before the two armies had a chance to combine forces against him. In order to provoke Flaminius, Hannibal began destroying area villages and land. The Roman senate considered Arretium a valuable asset, and Hannibal hoped its destruction would enrage Flaminius to the point that he would leave his post. Though he ravaged the countryside, Flaminius stood his ground without being goaded. Hannibal then marched south of Flaminius's army in an extremely bold move, leaving himself vulnerable to attack from behind. Hannibal moved south towards Lake Trasimene, and, despite advice to remain at his post, Flaminius gave in and pursued Hannibal.

The Carthaginians made camp on the northeast shores of the lake. During the night, Hannibal quickly moved most of his troops onto the hills overlooking the north shore of the lake. He had some soldiers light campfires far away from where his army was camped, in order to confuse the Romans as to their actual position. The following morning, the hills surrounding Lake Trasimene were covered in mist. The Romans approached the lake and saw the smaller number of Carthage soldiers on the far shore. The Romans were tricked into thinking this small regiment was evidence of vastly reduced troops in the process of flight. As they rapidly encroached upon Hannibal's visible soldiers, war cries began to ring out from the surrounding hilltops. Hannibal's perched soldiers charged the shore from above, screaming as they came. Again, trickery and the element of surprise allowed Hannibal to employ the perfect ensnarement. It was one of the largest ambushes in ancient warfare. The Romans, who were confused and did not have their weapons drawn, were not in fighting formation, and their vision was obscured by the fog that had yet to dissipate. To make matters worse for Rome, the Carthaginians were traveling swiftly downhill towards them. This limited confusion for Hannibal's troops, and despite also being affected by limited visibility, the Carthage soldiers knew that anyone in front of them during their descent was probably an enemy.

Hannibal's mass of Iberians, Africans, and Gauls flew towards the Romans, screaming in several different languages, throwing stones, and hurling javelins from above. When they reached the Roman soldiers, they fought by hand and spear, completely overwhelming the unsuspecting soldiers. Many Romans were pushed into the lake in the process of retreat, and thousands drowned. Flaminius was killed in a confrontation with the Gauls on the shore of Lake Trasimene that lasted over three hours. The Romans had also lost fifteen thousand other soldiers. As for Hannibal, he had lost 2,500 soldiers, and the funeral pyres burned high and long on the shores of Lake Trasimene. When the battle ended, Hannibal had managed to leave Servilius behind him as he traveled south. This left Carthage's multinational fighting force closer to Rome's gates than any of the Roman soldiers who had been sent to stop him.

The Battle of Cannae

After discovering that one consul had been killed, Rome decided to appoint a dictator to command the military as opposed to replacing a consul. Hannibal had been taking advantage of Rome's strategy of splitting their overall fighting force between two commanders, and the Romans hoped a dictator would put an end to this. They selected Quintus Fabius Maximus Verrucosus Cunctator to the position. Maximus was a Roman aristocrat who knew that Hannibal's army might be superior to Roman forces, thus he planned to avoid battle by cutting off the Carthaginians from essential supplies and otherwise hampering the opposing army. Maximus's war of **attrition** worked in the sense that no battles were lost to Hannibal, but the Carthage army burned Roman property, killed Romans, and laid siege to Roman territory. Rome began to become bloodthirsty for revenge in battle. After six months of Maximus's dictatorship, Rome elected two new consuls and drafted an army twice the size of its former fighting force.

In June of 216 BCE, Hannibal captured the city of Cannae, allowing his army to access many supplies. Cannae was a Roman storage depot that proved invaluable to the Carthaginians. This rendered the Roman war of attrition irrelevant. Rome had assembled eighty-eight thousand soldiers who were now ready for battle. In late July, Rome sent its two new consuls, Gaius

Terentius Varro and Aemilius Paulus, and its entire army to Cannae. Rome still expected the consuls to maintain equal power even though they were now fighting alongside each other. The balance of power was to be upheld by each consul commanding the whole army on alternating days. This had the potential to create chaos if the consuls had different strategies and the whole military at the mercy of their will half the time. According to Polybius, these consuls had opposite demeanors. Varro was described as being more reckless and impulsive while Paulus seemed to be the more levelheaded of the two.

Upon arriving in Cannae, the Romans seemed to have the

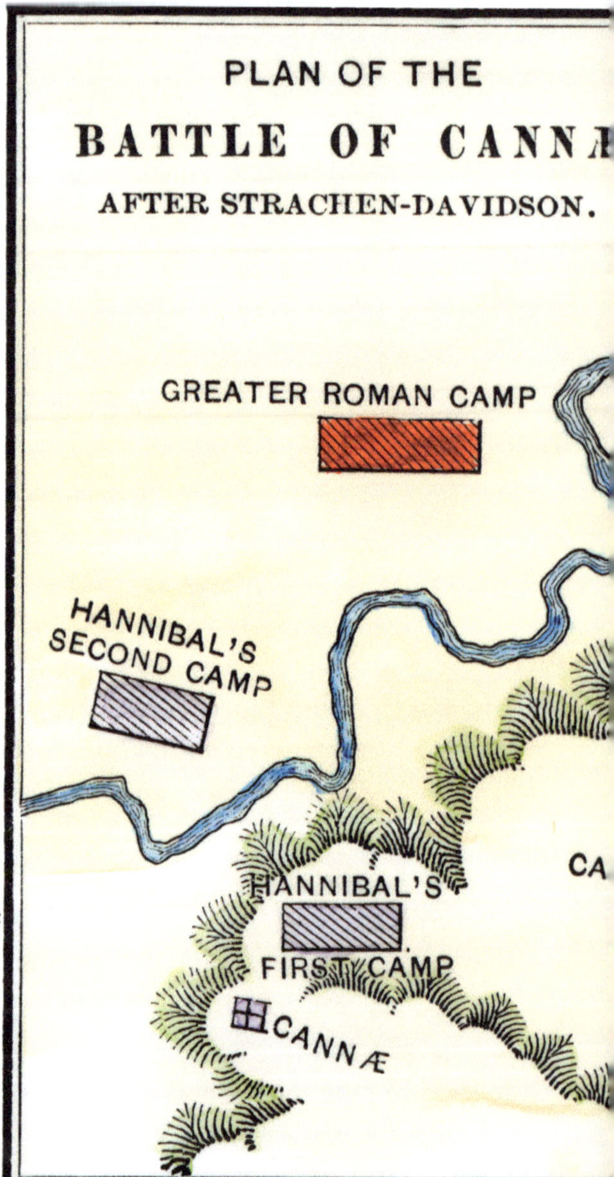

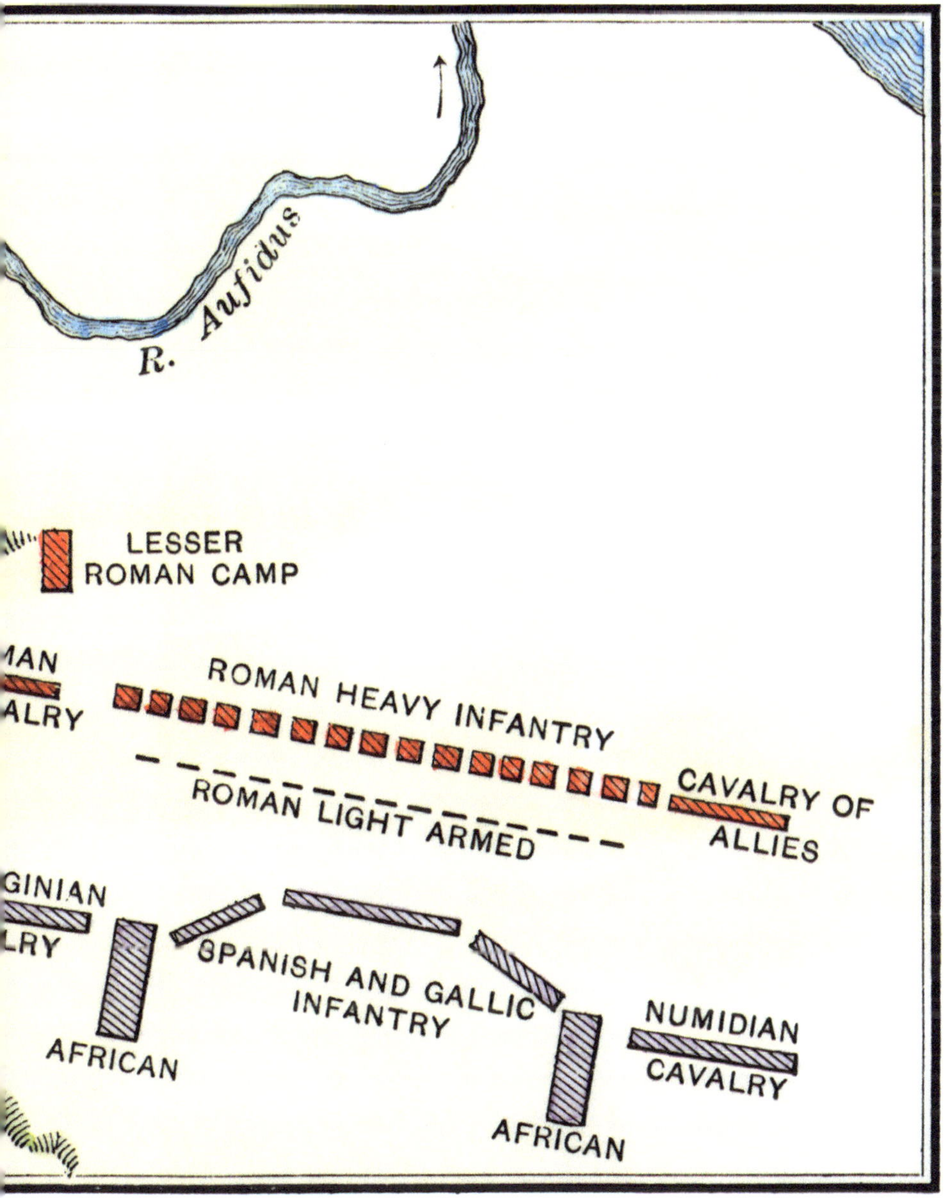

Hannibal was vastly outnumbered at the Battle of Cannae but used his flanking cavalries to manipulate Roman battle formations.

DEADLY SLINGSHOT

Though his ambushes were key in securing defeat against his enemy, Hannibal relied heavily upon the weaponry and training of his army in battle. One of Hannibal's greatest assets was his Balearic slingers. These troops hailed from the Balearic Islands situated in the western Mediterranean and spent years mastering their weapon of choice. These ancient woven firearms could launch a projectile more than 1,500 feet (457 m), a longer range than a bow and arrow. The Balearic slings were said to be made of rush, a grass-like plant that grows near wetlands. The sling required a very long training period, as it required greater skill than the point-and-shoot bow and arrow. Balearic slingers trained intensively from early childhood. Balearic parents gifted their children with a sling as their very first toy. When the child was old enough to be familiar with the sling, parents would place a piece of bread on a pole and withhold meals until the child could knock the bread from the pole with a missile. Balearic slingers mastered three different sizes of slings in order to be able to launch objects a variety of distances. They even engraved their projectiles, made of lead or stone, with their names or messages for their unlucky enemies. Hannibal brought more than a thousand Balearic slingers with him on his campaign against Rome and was fond of situating them ahead of his main infantry to interfere with Roman front lines. He did this at the Battle of Trebbia and the Battle of Cannae with much success.

Opposite: Balearic slingers were among the most skilled and well studied of Hannibal's multinational fighting force.

advantage because their army were almost twice the size of Hannibal's military. Nevertheless, the approaching Romans were impressed by the multinational fighting force. Many of Hannibal's soldiers wore Roman armor as a result of their recent victories. As Hannibal led his army onto the fields of Cannae at the beginning of August, Paulus surveyed the Carthaginian position and decided not to engage Hannibal. The next day, under Varro's control, the Roman army marched to the battlefield along the banks of the Aufidius River. The two armies proceeded to assume battle formations.

While the Romans opted for their traditional formation of three solid lines, Hannibal knew that his smaller army would not be able to sustain a head-on attack. Hannibal's cavalry had been proven superior to Rome's, and he decided to rely on these units once again. He formed the soldiers into a crescent shape with the arch of the crescent facing the Romans. With the center of the Carthaginian line bowed slightly, Hannibal placed his cavalry forces at either end of the crescent, flanking the infantry. Again, Hannibal worked to draw the Romans into a strategic position. As the strong Roman center pushed forward against Carthage's crescent, Hannibal's middle infantry began to move slowly backwards, drawing the Roman closer and closer. At the same time, the flanking forces continued to move in on the Romans. The crescent was effectively reversed with the arch bowing out away from the Romans. Without being aware, the Romans had once again fallen for Hannibal's tactic of controlled retreat. As the Roman formation deteriorated, the left flank of the Carthage cavalry closest to the river scored a major victory against the Romans. They were able to circle behind the Roman lines and then attack the right Roman flank furthest from the river. The Roman cavalry fled, leaving the infantry exposed. Hannibal's men were then able to completely encompass the Romans who were trapped, formless, and fighting without direction. The battle became a massacre, with anywhere from fifty thousand to seventy thousand Romans dying in a single day. The 2-mile (3.2 km) long, 3-mile (4.8 km) wide battlefield was littered with the bodies of killed and wounded Roman soldiers. Some Romans were said to have been found dead with their heads buried in the sandy banks of the river, something they seemed to have done in shock. Paulus was killed; Varro escaped but was disgraced by the slaughter.

The Battle of Cannae stands as the most conclusive victory in the ancient world. It shocked Rome and the Mediterranean world into recognizing Carthage as a formidable power. Only around fourteen thousand Romans managed to escape Cannae with their lives, and most of them were taken prisoner by Hannibal. Hannibal's innovative strategy is still studied by military academies around the world today as the standard for battles of envelopment. Cannae is Hannibal's signature victory, and although he seemed to be on the road to successfully fulfilling his father's wish of defeating Rome, a Roman son would soon rise up with visions of vengeance all his own.

CHAPTER FOUR

The Aftermath *of* Cannae

The Battle of Cannae was Hannibal's most decisive victory against the Romans and remains one of the most inspiring examples of strategic military excellence and cunning in the history of warfare. Rome had never suffered such a catastrophic loss. However, Hannibal would find himself continually hampered by limited resources and make several false assumptions in the wake of victory that would eventually lead to Carthage's downfall and Rome's ascension to the most powerful empire in the ancient world.

Hannibal Hesitates

Livy tells us that a Carthaginian general named Maharbol implored Hannibal to capitalize on the victory at Cannae and take the fight to Rome since the road to the republic's gates was open. Hannibal was concerned about reinforcements. Carthage had resisted coming to Hannibal's aid in terms of supplies and manpower, placing the burden of raising and maintaining a competent military squarely on Hannibal's shoulders. Thus,

Opposite: Hordes of Roman soldiers were killed at the Battle of Cannae, one of the most impressive displays of military strategy in the history of warfare.

Hannibal chose to spend his time and energy focused on persuading Italian settlements to abandon their allegiance to Rome and join his cause.

In the aftermath of Cannae, Hannibal sent emissaries to Rome in order to collect ransom for his hostages and negotiate terms of surrender. Rome was resolute even in the face of incredible defeat. Ten hostages accompanied the emissaries, but Rome not only refused to pay for their return, the senate also outlawed Roman families from paying any ransom for their captive relatives. Hannibal's men returned empty-handed, shocking the battle-worn general.

Instead of bowing to Carthage, Rome set about replenishing their decimated army. An even more massive force was assembled with twenty-five legions of four thousand men each. Rome relaxed its standards for enlistment and allowed boys to serve. Rome promised slaves who enlisted their freedom and allowed criminals and debtors to join the ranks. The war tax was also increased in order to secure funds for equipment and rations. As time passed, it became apparent that Hannibal was not planning on storming Rome immediately, and the morale of the army improved. Rome's access to manpower was one of the most frustrating aspects of the Second Punic War for Hannibal. Despite astounding victories, he continued to face a massive, renewable military.

Hannibal began making his way through southern Italy, attempting to sway Italians to join the fight. He was successful in securing Capua, an important coastal city, as well as Syracuse on the island of Sicily. Hannibal also managed to sign a treaty with the king of Macedon, who promised to send another army to assist in the coming battle with Rome. Despite these significant gains, the majority of Italians could not be pressured to take up the fight. In the words of Livy, "Not one Roman citizen nor one Latin community had joined Hannibal."

Rome was concerned about Hannibal's recruitment campaign and sought to fortify as many cities as possible. They were especially troubled about the loss of Syracuse because it put them in danger of losing Sicily, a treasured trading post in the western Mediterranean. Once the soldiers were fully trained, the bulk of the Roman army and the veterans of Cannae were sent to Sicily to safeguard against an invasion.

Rome Resumes War of Attrition

After Cannae, Rome realized it had been too quick to abandon its war of attrition against Hannibal and focused once again on cutting the Carthaginian forces off from necessary resources. They ordered farmers in Roman territories to harvest their crops and send them to areas that were not vulnerable to Hannibal, in order to keep the Carthaginians from confiscating rations to feed their army. Roman fleets were also dispatched to monitor both coasts of Italy, and another fleet was sent to patrol the Sicilian coast. The units stationed near the Italian coast intercepted a Greek vessel, boarded the ship, and discovered the reinforcements that the king of Macedon had promised Hannibal. The Romans also engaged with skirmishes across Italy in an attempt to put down resistance to the republic. One engagement was with the citizens of Capua. Many were killed, sending a message to those that might consider abandoning Rome. While securing Italian territories, Rome also branched out and began occupying areas where the Carthaginian army did not have a presence. Though they sought to avoid battle with Hannibal, Rome had no problem asserting its authority in other locales. One of these was the island of Sardinia.

No Assistance from Carthage

After Cannae, Hannibal sent Mago to Carthage with rings taken from the hands of the Roman soldiers as proof of Hannibal's successes. Mago poured mounds of the jewelry out on the floor of the senate in an impressive display and asked for reinforcements to continue the fight. Astonishingly, the Carthaginian senate refused and instead sent reinforcements to Spain. It is generally believed that the decision not to support the war effort was motivated by political rivalry. Hannibal's menace in the senate was a senator named Hanno. Rome did not suffer from such infighting, and political rivalries were set aside for the good of the republic. Once Roman occupation reached the shores of Sardinia, the Carthage senate was once again called upon to send reinforcements for protection. Carthage supplied some backup, but the Romans still dominated in battle. In two decisive victories, Rome killed or captured five thousand Carthaginians and gained control of Sardinia.

Meanwhile, Rome had retained its core allies in north and central Italy. Hannibal's strategy depended upon Italian desertion of Rome, and as time went on, it became clear that this might not come to pass. Roman allies that had defected to Hannibal were becoming concerned as the Roman armies went about securing territories and punishing resistance. They turned to Hannibal and called for protection. Without outside assistance, Hannibal was forced to attempt to assuage these fears on his own and was distracted from the task of developing a focused strategy to defeat Rome.

At the Gates of Rome

As Roman forces were bolstered, they fortified more and more Italian cities and eventually set their sights on regaining control of Capua. In 218 BCE they laid siege to the valuable supply depot. Hannibal knew Capua was vital to sustaining his military and made a bold decision to attempt to draw the Romans away from the city by marching his men straight to the gates

As Hannibal laid siege to Roman territories, Rome gained control of Hannibal's supply depots, forcing Hannibal to march to Rome's gates.

of Rome. He camped outside Rome's walls as the city quaked in fear of Carthaginian invasion. The Romans did not attempt to remove Hannibal with force, and Hannibal did not have an adequate military to lay siege to the powerful republic. Eventually, Hannibal was forced to retreat to southeast Italy, becoming a consistent but manageable nuisance to the Romans.

War Comes to Carthage

In 206 BCE, Publius Cornelius Scipio was elected to become a commander in Rome's army. His father had been wounded in battle with Hannibal, and Scipio the Younger had fought against Hannibal throughout the Second Punic War including the Battle of Cannae. He was well-versed on Hannibal's preferred tactics and strategies. While Hannibal was contained in southern Italy, Scipio proceeded to conquer all of Spain in the name of Rome, effectively waging the same kind of war that Hannibal had hoped to wage in Italy. Scipio was elected consul and granted rule over Sicily, where he reunited with other veterans from the battle of Cannae. Two years later, Scipio and an army of seventeen thousand set sail from Sicily to Northern Africa. Through his defeat of Spain, Scipio had managed to acquire units of Numidian cavalry, the same forces that had served Hannibal so well in former battles against Rome. When Scipio arrived in Carthage, he wreaked havoc, and the Carthaginian senate was forced to send word to Hannibal to return home after nine years of fighting without major victory in southern Italy.

In 203 BCE, Hannibal reached the shores of North Africa with an army of fifteen thousand soldiers. About a third of his fighting force was composed of veterans while the rest were lesser-trained recruits. Upon arrival, Scipio and Hannibal meet outside the city of Zama. Though we have no way of knowing what the two said to each other, they must have had great mutual respect. In the words of Livy, "They were not only the two greatest soldiers of their time but the equals of any king or commander in the whole of the world." The generals did not come to peace terms despite whatever admiration they held for each other. Both retired to prepare their respective armies for the coming conflict.

Battle of Zama

With Scipio's recent acquisition of Numidian cavalry forces, Hannibal was for the first time in his military career facing a superior cavalry. Carthage had managed to supply him with eighty elephants. He knew that he would have to rely on the elephants if he was to have any hope of victory. Both armies were formed into three lines. Hannibal positioned his elephants in the center of the front line. He placed his least-experienced troops furthest to the front while his veterans occupied the third line of attack. Hannibal's plan was to use the elephants to trample the enemy and follow with an attack by his infantry. However, Scipio was prepared for this strategy and commanded his men to form lanes allowing the elephants to charge straight through Roman lines without trampling soldiers. This severely reduced the effectiveness of Hannibal's strategy. As the battle got underway, the opposing cavalries clashed. The Carthaginians began to break and flee, but Scipio had seen Hannibal's hit-and-run strategies before and could not be certain if he was being coaxed into a trap. The cavalries continued to clash on the wings of battle as the infantry prepared to engage.

As Scipio's army advanced, the three Roman lines suddenly reformed into a single solid line of Roman resistance. The

Romans were then able to swiftly decimate the first line of Carthaginians. The second line of Hannibal's army was crushed soon after, leaving just the third line. As the Romans faced off against Hannibal's veterans, the fighting took on a new tone. Many of Scipio's soldiers were veterans from the Battle of Cannae, and those who were not had certainly been informed of the crushing defeat Hannibal had dealt Rome. Hannibal's remaining soldiers were the same men who had orchestrated that defeat. The old wounds that had been inflicted fourteen years earlier were thus reopened in a vicious settling of old scores.

Just as Rome's infantry was reaching Hannibal's third line, the Roman cavalry returned from pursuit of Hannibal's cavalry and

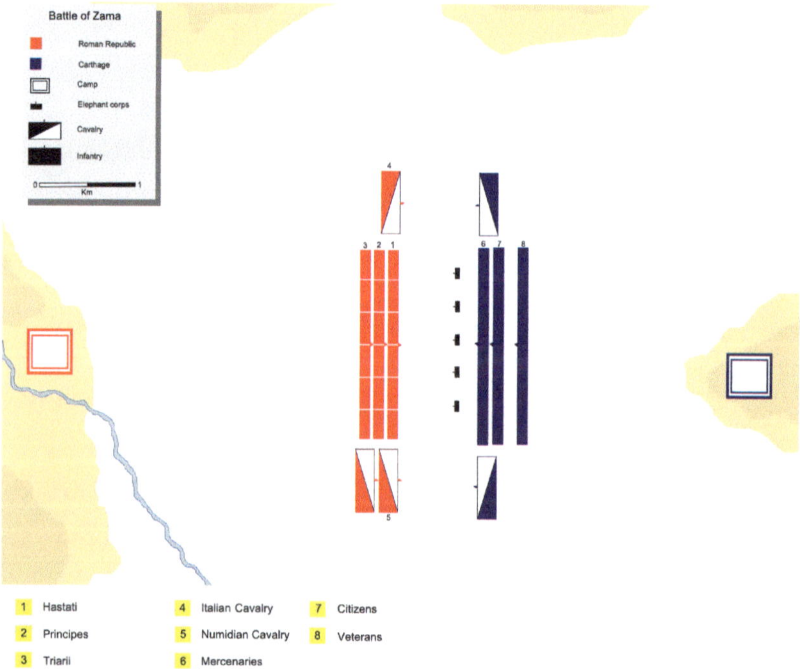

In a detrimental reversal, Roman strategy relied heavily on cavalry forces to manipulate Hannibal's well-planned troop formation during the Battle of Zama.

managed to circle behind Hannibal's army, pinning the dwindling force between Roman assaults. This overwhelmed Hannibal's army and secured Scipio's victory against the man who had seriously wounded his father. Scipio employed exactly the same strategies to defeat Carthage as Hannibal had used in victories against Rome.

More than two thousand Carthaginians were killed when the Battle of Zama came to a close, and almost as many soldiers were taken prisoner by Scipio's army. Scipio's victory earned him the new moniker Scipio Africanus in honor of defeating the powerful North African, Hannibal, and the city of Carthage. He was the first Roman general to take a name from the very people he had conquered.

The Surrender of Carthage

After the Battle of Zama, Carthage was forced to submit to Rome. The terms of surrender offered by Rome included giving up all claims to land under Roman occupation, surrendering their elephants and what was left of the Carthage navy, and paying reparations to Rome. Carthage was also forbidden to wage war with anyone without the express permission of Rome. Scipio was lenient in his treatment of Carthage in the aftermath of Zama. He was eager to return to Rome and bask in the glory of having brought peace to Rome and beaten the feared Hannibal. These desires compelled him to offer terms of surrender that were somewhat merciful. He also allowed Hannibal to go free and return to Carthage. This act, possibly more than any other, strengthened the myth of Hannibal in Roman imaginations.

Even after Hannibal's defeat at the Battle of Zama, the Roman Senate still sought revenge against both the Carthaginian general and the city-state itself.

Hannibal's Final Years

In 201 BCE, with the Second Punic War over, Hannibal returned to Carthage, a city he hadn't seen since he was nine years old. Five years after returning, Hannibal became another kind of leader: a politician. He was elected chief magistrate. His focus was on eliminating corruption in the Carthaginian government, and he set about enacting several reforms. Within a few years, Carthage gathered funds to pay the first installment of the hefty indemnity they owed to Rome.

Livy tells us that this payment caused the Carthage senate much grief and as senators wept at the thought of supplying Rome with riches, Hannibal laughed. After being reprimanded, Hannibal responded, "… the time to weep was when our arms were taken from us, our ships were burnt and we were forbidden foreign wars. That was when we received our deathblow …" Hannibal must have been incredibly frustrated to see the very men who had refused to support his successful military campaign weeping at the results of their inaction.

Hannibal's political adversaries would later betray him to the Romans. Messengers were sent to Rome to spread rumor of Hannibal planning to mount another offensive assault on the republic. With fear of Hannibal still living in the hearts and minds of the Roman people, Rome sent envoys to arrest the former general. Upon discovering that he has been betrayed, Hannibal fled Carthage and never returned.

Hannibal swiftly resumed his pursuit of victory against Rome and sought refuge in Syria, where King Antiochus was engaged in war with Rome. Immediately, Hannibal was given command of naval forces and appointed chief military advisor. Though Carthage had been known for its naval prowess, Hannibal had spent his military career waging war on land using territorial strategy and psychological tactics to defeat his enemies. In engaging battle at sea, there were no such opportunities for him to take superior position or launch surprise attacks. Hannibal was unable to adapt his style of fighting to the demands of naval warfare, and the Romans overwhelmingly defeated King Antiochus. Upon victory, Rome once again demanded Hannibal be delivered to Roman authorities. Hannibal fled once more. Rome would pursue Hannibal for the rest of his life, motivated by the fear that the once-great Carthaginian general would someday rise to the command of another army and continually seek revenge against Rome.

In 183 BCE, Roman forces finally closed in upon Hannibal. In Bithynia, near the southern coast of the Black Sea, Hannibal was betrayed by King Prusias, who shared his location with Rome. Upon hearing the news of Rome's approach, Hannibal mixed a poison and killed himself in his chambers. Much like his father before him, Hannibal chose suicide over death at the hand of his captors. He was in his sixties at the time of his death and had spent the majority of his life in battle with Rome. Suicide allowed him to avoid the indignity of giving Rome the satisfaction of his capture.

The Third Punic War

Hannibal's death set the stage for Carthage's ultimate disaster. Rome and Carthage would go on to fight a Third Punic War, which would end in 146 BCE with the total destruction of Carthage. Carthage's conflict with neighboring Numidians resulted in the city squaring off with Scipio the Younger once more. In the end, Carthage was burned to the ground. It is said among historians that Romans were so ruthless in their erasure of Carthage that they sowed the land with salt to be sure nothing could grow from the plots where Carthage had once stood. With the defeat of its once formidable foe, Rome continued to expand from an Italian city-state to a gargantuan empire that would dominate the world for the next five hundred years.

A Debt Paid

At the end of the Second Punic War, Carthage had been ordered to pay an indemnity to Rome for fifty years. Once again, Carthage was able to rejuvenate their wealth with help from Hannibal's time as suffete. They managed to stay in Rome's good graces by paying their debts and blaming the Second Punic War on Hannibal's independent campaign against Rome. During the period following the close of the Second Punic War, the Numidians, formerly allied neighbors to Carthage, began encroaching on territory that had once belonged to the Mediterranean city-state. As the fifty-year period came to a close, the Carthaginians sought to make war with Numidia. In 150 BCE, Carthage sent an army of about thirty thousand men to wage war with their neighbor, but the battle turned out to be a slaughter for the Carthaginians with the Numidians triumphing easily. Worse yet, Carthage had sworn that it would not make war without the express permission of Rome as part of the peace treaty that ended the Second Punic War. Rome now had a reason to resume battle with its old adversary. One Roman in particular, a senator named Marcus Porcius Cato, or Cato the Elder, had seen Carthage's economic rebirth and set about arguing for the annihilation of the once equally powerful enemy. Cato regularly spoke of the need for Carthage's demise. He would doggedly demand "Carthage must be destroyed" whenever he addressed the Roman senate. In 149 BCE, Cato's wish was granted.

Rome Makes War

Although Carthage attempted to reassure the Romans by sending messengers to Rome with orders to explain the cause and reasons for their conflict with Numidia, Rome was not interested in listening. With many Romans still sore from Hannibal's humiliating victories over them in the Second Punic War, another war with Carthage was not just looked at as a necessity but an opportunity for revenge. Those members of the Roman senate who may have been slow to recommend war on Carthage were convinced when Utica, a former ally of Carthage, pledged its allegiance to Rome. With that, the Romans had a nearby harbor that would allow for an accessible path of invasion into Carthage. Rome declared war and sent an army of about eighty thousand infantry and four thousand cavalry to the shores of North Africa.

When Rome's army reached Carthage, they commanded the Carthaginians to surrender at once. Carthage was ordered to disband its military, surrender all weapons, and release its prisoners. In addition, the citizens of Carthage were told to leave the walls of the city and resettle elsewhere. With few options, Carthage prepared to stand and fight. Thirty thousand troops were called back to Carthage from Numidia, and the two hundred thousand Carthaginians within the fortified city readied themselves for battle.

Carthage Under Siege

With the decision to take a stand, Carthaginians scrambled, using all their resources to make weapons in preparation for the coming onslaught. In two months, they managed to produce six thousand shields, eighteen thousand swords, thirty thousand spears, and one hundred and twenty ships. With their mass of weapons and

This illustration depicts the carnage that ensued once Roman forces breached the walls of Carthage.

the walls of Carthage, they were able to hold off the Romans for three long years. The Romans were eventually able to breach the city by using the harbor as a point of entry. Even after they penetrated the outer wall, it took the Roman army another week to reach the top of the massive third wall surrounding Carthage. Once the Romans were inside, ruthless, chaotic fighting filled the streets of Carthage. This went on for about a week before Romans set about burning the city to the ground. The Roman army set Carthage ablaze, district by district. Only fifty thousand Carthaginians survived the flames, which burned for seventeen days. The scorch marks can still be seen on some of the ruins at the site of ancient Carthage. Survivors were sold into slavery, and the culture and viewpoints of Carthage were lost with the destruction of their temples, libraries, and other sacred buildings.

Rome After Carthage

Rome changed in many ways as a result of the Punic Wars. The Senate became much more powerful as citizens now considered the senate as the authority in terms of declaring and executing violence against other nations. The Second Punic War left fertile land in Italy widely available. Former inhabitants had been killed during the war or had sought the safety of more populated areas. The number of prisoners of Rome skyrocketed, and as a result, Rome became economically dependent upon slavery. While these changes seemed at first to serve the growth and prosperity of Rome, they eventually led to serious problems within the republic.

Poverty and Overcrowding

Italians who had once owned farmland in the Po Valley and elsewhere began moving to more populated cities during and after the Punic Wars. A drop in the price of grain shortly after the Punic Wars led many farmers to migrate to Rome and other more populated areas. Veterans and families flocked to ancient cities, and, as this trend continued, Rome became the most populated city in Europe. New inhabitants would have seen a very different life than they had been accustomed to on rural farms. The luxurious draw of ancient Rome would have been a departure from the daily toil of farm life. As Rome became more embroiled in military conquest and the population grew, various forms of entertainment were plentiful. A variety of public spectacles occupied the interests of the war-worn republic. Some of these events, such as the funerals of aristocrats, victory processions, and banquets, took place in the streets of Rome. Other forms of entertainment demanded that structures be built to house spectators. Theaters were built for plays and other performances, chariot races were held in what is referred to as a **circus**, sports facilities called **stadia** were built to house athletic competitions, and of course, amphitheaters were constructed to house bloodsports such as battles that pitted gladiators against each other as well as against different beasts. Sometimes these arenas were even flooded in order to accommodate naval battles for entertainment. These forms of amusement were often bloody and allowed the aristocratic elite a variety of platforms for self-promotion. These events also helped citizens to feel pride in shared values and their Roman institutions. Most importantly, spectacle distracted the Roman people from the republic's almost constant state of war and also diverted their attention away from their own poverty.

Slavery

The Punic Wars and the ruin of Carthage had resulted in Rome acquiring at least seventy-five thousand slaves. As astounding

as that number is, many more were brought to Rome in the aftermath of other conflicts abroad. Rome's dependence upon slave labor grew. Cheap Italian farmland was bought up by wealthy Romans; some were former landowners who were looking to expand their properties, while others were businessmen looking for new investments in the wake of war. Larger and larger farms began to crop up, and more lands became vineyards and orchards. Both ranching and farming accommodated more than three hundred acres of southern and central Italian soil, the most affected area of the Second Punic War. Small farmers were soon unable to compete with new, larger operations that were run by dozens of slaves. Farmers who had once been the mainstay of the Roman economy were now poor city dwellers. Thousands of slaves poured into the city and were bought and sold on a daily basis. Romans were more expensive than other slaves such as Gauls and Spaniards. Male slaves were locked in underground prisons, worked under harsh supervision during the day, and shackled at night. Romans were considered wealthy if they had around ten slaves, and slavery became a basic part of everyday life in Rome. As Roman slavery **proliferated** within and outside of the republic, slaves escaped and traveled the countryside, surviving by thievery, which made leaving the confines of Rome hazardous. Slaves also revolted, leading Rome into another series of violent engagements.

Increased Focus on War

With the growth of the Roman Empire and large slave operations producing Roman goods abroad, the problem of revolts **vexed** Rome. The Servile Wars began in Sicily in 134 BCE. A Syrian

Opposite: As Rome became more dependent on slave labor, slave revolts increased both abroad and at home, as pictured here.

THE WRITINGS OF POLYBIUS

The Greek historian Polybius is our best source of information regarding Hannibal's life and campaigns. Polybius's account is not only the oldest surviving record, his connections with the relatives of Scipio Africanus also allowed him to travel the routes that Hannibal is believed to have taken and interview soldiers who had fought with and against the Carthaginian. Polybius's writing is *digressive* at times, but his descriptions of Hannibal's challenges and successes are riveting. This passage concerning Hannibal's trek through the Alps as the soldiers contend with fallen snow is an excellent example of Polybius's engaging narrative.

> The state of matters was altogether peculiar and unusual. The new snow which had fallen on the top of the old snow remaining since the previous winter, was itself yielding, both owing to its softness, being a fresh fall, and because it was not yet very deep, but when they had trodden through it and set foot on the congealed snow beneath it, they no longer sunk in it, but slid along it with both feet, as happens to those who walk on ground with a coat of mud on it. But what followed on this was even more trying. As for the men, when, unable to pierce the lower layer of snow, they fell and then tried to help themselves to rise by the support of their knees and hands, they slid along still more rapidly on these, the slope being exceedingly steep. But the animals, when they fell, broke through the lower layer of snow in their efforts to rise, and remained there with their packs as if frozen into it, owing to their weight and the congealed condition of this old snow. Giving up this project, then, Hannibal encamped on the ridge, sweeping it clear of snow, and next set the soldiers to work to build up the path along the cliff, a most toilsome task.

slave named Eunus led a group of about four hundred slaves to revolt, and they killed most of their masters. The success of the upheaval encouraged other Sicilian slaves to join Eunus, and eventually the slave army grew to around seventy thousand. Several Sicilian towns were taken by the slaves, and slave owners were massacred throughout the island. The revolt was eventually subdued, but three years passed and twenty thousand slaves were crucified before order was restored. This was also not the last insurrection that Rome would face. In the following years, Rome would be forced to devote military power to suppressing rebellions throughout its newly won territories, making it even more dependent upon the senate and its military to settle disputes through violence. The Second Servile War was fought in Sicily in 104 BCE, and it took the Romans four years to regain control of the region. A Third Servile War occurred on the mainland in 73 BCE. Meanwhile, the influx of slave labor continued, and Rome's economy was polarized by the contrast of incredibly wealthy slaveholding aristocrats and poverty-stricken free Romans.

The Legacy of Carthage

With Carthage destroyed, the culture, history, and writings of its citizens were lost to the ages. Though Carthage would rise again, it would be under the rule of Rome, so only a shadow of ancient Carthage remains. What we know of Hannibal and Carthage comes to us from the writings of Roman and Greek historians. It is hard to know where the line between man and myth exists with regard to Hannibal. Though he was focused on ridding his government of corruption and had shown Roman adversaries dignity in death, he is often portrayed as a merciless, military tyrant fueled by bloodthirst and greed.

CHAPTER FIVE

Hannibal's Myth Through *the* Ages

While Hannibal's incredible military pursuits and successes have been studied and revered throughout the ages, much of what we know about Hannibal has been handed down by cultures that were enemies of Carthage. After Rome's decimation of the ancient city-state, little was left for modern archaeologists and historians to study in order to piece together an accurate representation of Carthage or its greatest military leader. Only a handful of accurate recordings that detail Hannibal's life exist today. One thing is clear, Hannibal's reputation lived on long after he took his own life, and his very name was used to strike fear into the hearts of the Roman people.

Hannibal in the Roman Imagination

When Hannibal marched his army to the gates of Rome in order to draw the Roman army away from Carthage's Italian allies,

Opposite: The dramatic elements of Hannibal's legacy have been explored in both television programs and major motion pictures.

the citizens of Rome were terrified. The men took up fighting positions while the women, in keeping with Roman customs in times of attack, holed up in the temples and swept the floors of their shrines with their hair. In their panic, they prayed to the gods for protection from the fierce Carthaginian general. Eventually Rome defeated both Hannibal and Carthage, but the fear Hannibal had engendered would forever be associated with his name. It became customary for Romans to call out, "Hannibal is at the gates!" whenever Rome faced a pressing threat. Hannibal even served as a kind of bogeyman for children. Roman mothers would warn their children that if they didn't behave, Hannibal would snatch them up in the night. His name is still used today as a symbol of a surprise but very real threat that is capable of destroying even the most powerful.

In a sense, Hannibal made the Roman Empire possible. Once Rome had completely defeated Hannibal and Carthage, it found itself with the most powerful military in the world. Rome had at its disposal an unmatched navy and a massive army whose generals had faced a frustrating and deadly test in their battles with Hannibal. After Hannibal's death, the legend of his life took on a rather strange significance for Rome. As the empire grew stronger and stronger, Rome found fewer and fewer worthy adversaries. The memorialization of the one general who had posed a real threat to the empire became more important to supporting Rome's ideal of itself as a great and powerful empire.

Hannibal in Modern Imagination

Hannibal has inspired much admiration and contemplation since his death. Artists have depicted his crossing of the Alps and his numerous battles against Rome, and poets have written about his exploits. Major motion pictures and numerous documentaries have been filmed in an effort to share the general's life with the contemporary public. While interest in Hannibal is no doubt spurred by what is known of Hannibal's amazing feats, it is also owed in part to how little is known for sure about the great man's life.

Visual Art

Visual artists have been moved to depict various scenes in Hannibal's life. From his oath to be an enemy of Rome to his crossing of the Alps, the following paintings act as graphic musings on the legacy of Hannibal.

Hannibal Crossing the Alps

Scenes of Hannibal and his army traversing the harsh Alps have been painted by a variety of artists. In this Heinrich Leutemann painting, done in 1866, the viewer's eye wanders from the foreground of elephants and soldiers desperate to ascend the mountain to the background where, as the army climbs, they are attacked by hostile tribes and some soldiers as well as elephants fall to their deaths as they reach the peak.

The Oath of Hannibal

The scene in which Hannibal joins his father at the sacrificial altar and swears to be a lifelong enemy to Rome is perhaps the most iconic and well-known scene of Hannibal's life. In this 1770 painting by Benjamin West, Carthaginians point and gossip as Hamilcar encourages a cautious Hannibal to place his hand on a

Hannibal's oath of enmity to Rome at the request of his father, as imagined here by Benjamin West, is integral to his mythology.

bull readied for sacrifice. The impending moment depicted in a shadowy temple gives the painting a particularly eerie quality. The decision to portray young Hannibal as hesitant is interesting considering that it is generally told that Hannibal was enthusiastic about the invitation to join his father in Spain.

Hannibal Looks at the Head of Hasdrubal

Another gut-wrenching visual detail about Hannibal's life is the fact that his brother's corpse was decapitated by the Romans who defeated him and delivered to Hannibal's camp, where it was flung over the walls as a sign of utter disrespect and certain defeat for Carthage. In this eighteenth-century painting, Giambattista Tiepolo imagines what that moment must have looked like. The shadowy cave where Hannibal stands is contrasted by the bright blue sky outside his sanctuary. Similarly, Hannibal is seen recoiling in shock at the sight of his brother's head while soldiers outside his cave seem to fight back the Romans. Showing the brave Carthaginian in a moment of horror creates an interesting juxtaposition to the myth of Hannibal as being unshakable.

Literature

Much has been written about the Punic Wars and Hannibal's battles, and because writing was the most accessible art form in ancient times, authors began recording the legendary deeds of Hannibal not long after he died. Poets used his image both as a means of detailing the downfall of Carthage and as a metaphor. Hannibal is present in some of the most important works in the literary canon.

Virgil's *Aeneid*

Between the years of 29 BCE and 19 BCE, the poet Virgil wrote his epic poem the *Aeneid*, which follows the tale of Aeneas, an ancestor of Rome who begins the poem as a Trojan who travels to Italy. The poem serves as a sort of preamble to the rise of Rome. Virgil does not mention Hannibal by name but uses the character of Dido, the Queen who legend says founded Carthage, as a symbol for Carthage while Aeneas serves as a symbol for Rome. In the poem, Aeneas and Dido become lovers. Though Aeneas fears Dido, he is told by the god Jupiter that he must leave her. Aeneas slips away, and when Dido finds that her lover has left, she flies into a rage and kills herself. Before she ends her life, she makes an impassioned speech:

Giambattista Tiepolo illustrates the moment that Hannibal is confronted with the severed head of Hasdrubal in this painting.

> Then, O my Tyrians, besiege with hate his progeny and all his race to come: Make this your offering to my dust. No love, no pact must be between our peoples; No, but rise up from my bones, avenging spirit! Harry with fire and sword … Coast with coast in conflict, I implore, and sea with sea, and arms with arms: may they contend in war, themselves and all the children of their children!

The avenging spirit that Virgil mentions is almost certainly a reference to Hannibal, who at the time the *Aeneid* was penned still loomed large in Rome's memory as the greatest enemy the empire had faced. Later in the book, Virgil makes an even more explicit allusion to the Carthaginian general. During a meeting of the gods on Mount Olympus, Jupiter says: "The time for war will come—you need not press for it—that day when through the Alps laid open wide the savagery of Carthage blights the towns and towers of Rome."

The reference to the Alps can leave no doubt in the reader's mind that Virgil is talking about Hannibal's impending march on Rome.

Juvenal's Satires

Juvenal was a Roman poet who wrote sixteen satirical poems. Divided into five books, these poems fall into the **satire** tradition and serve as comedic critiques of society. Juvenal's Satires were written in the late first and early second century CE. Many popular **adages** of the English language are derived from Juvenal's work such as, "a sound mind in a sound body," and "Who will watch the watcher?" The tenth poem examines how humans sometimes desire that which is most dangerous to their well-being. Juvenal writes:

> Put Hannibal in the scales: how many pounds will that peerless
>
> General weigh today? A man for whom Africa
>
> Was too small a continent, though it stretched from the surf-beaten
>
> Ocean shores of Morocco east to the steamy Nile,
>
> To Ethiopian tribesmen—and new elephants' habitats
>
> Now Spain swells his empire, now he surmounts
>
> The Pyrenees, Nature throws in his path
>
> High Alpine passes, blizzards of snow: but he splits
>
> The very rocks asunder, moves mountains—with vinegar.
>
> Now Italy is his, yet still he forces on.

More than two centuries after Hannibal's death, Juvenal seems to suggest the Carthaginian general should have stopped while he was ahead and been glad for the accomplishments he was able to complete instead of pressing on to his eventual demise. In a harsher tone, Juvenal imagines how a defeated Hannibal may have looked:

> A fine sight it must have been,
>
> Fit subject for caricature, the one-eyed commander
>
> Perched on his monstrous beast! Alas, alas, for glory,

What an end was here: the defeat, the ignominious
Flight into exile, everyone crowding to see
The once-mighty Hannibal turned humble hanger-on,
Sitting outside the door of a petty Eastern despot

Satirists are successful in part due to their ability to evoke shock at that which they critique. Their observations are designed to make the average citizen uncomfortable. The fact that it would have shocked the citizens of Rome for a voice to call Hannibal's accomplishments into question and mock him in defeat so many years after his death is a testament to the longevity of his legacy and a twisted sign of respect for the enemy of Rome.

Flaubert's *Salammbô*

In the 1850s, the French writer Gustave Flaubert turned to ancient Carthage for inspiration for his next novel. The publication of his last novel, *Madame Bovary*, had led to an obscenity trial (Flaubert was eventually acquitted). *Madame Bovary* would become a classic text but *Salammbô*, his follow-up, is lesser known among English speakers. The historical novel was published in 1862 and set before and during the Mercenary Revolt, which took place shortly after the First Punic War, in which Hamilcar fought against soldiers he had once commanded. The titular character is an imagined daughter of Hamilcar, sister of Hannibal. Flaubert's surreal *Salammbô* is full of primal images of war and passion, but Hannibal, a young child at the time of the setting, is not leading Carthage's military campaign. Towards the end of the novel, Carthage is in a dire position as the mercenaries have gained control of Carthage's water supply. Children of Carthaginian elite are to be offered for sacrifice, but instead of sending his son out to die, Hamilcar disguises a young slave as Hannibal to be sacrificed in his place. Flaubert's **visceral** depiction of ancient Carthage does not centralize Hannibal's military career, but the choice to suppose that Hamilcar would spare his son's life is interesting. It is as if, even though his novel was a fictional creation in a historical setting, Flaubert knew he needed to save Hannibal in order for him to be available to challenge Rome. In any case, Flaubert, who researched Carthage obsessively during the writing of *Salammbô*, was drawn to the relationship between Hamilcar and Hannibal thousands of years after the events he wrote about took place.

Freud's *Interpretation of Dreams*

In 1899 Freud published his seminal *The Interpretation of Dreams*, which included an explanation of his theory of the unconscious and its influence on dreaming. A little over thirty years after Flaubert published his vision of ancient Carthage's decadence, Sigmund Freud divulged a fascination with the relationship between Hamilcar and Hannibal Barca. Freud describes how an anecdote shared with him by his father inspired his glorification of the Carthaginians' relationship.

> I may have been ten or twelve years old, when my father began to take me with him on his walks and reveal to me in his talk his views about things in the world we live in. Thus it was, on one such occasion, that he told me a story to show me how much better things were now than they had been in his days.

> "When I was a young man," he said, "I went for a walk one Saturday in the streets of your birthplace; I was well dressed, and had a new fur cap on my head. A Christian came up to me and with a single blow knocked off my cap into the mud and shouted: 'Jew! Get off the pavement!'"
>
> "And what did you do?" I asked. "I went into the roadway and picked up my cap," was his quiet reply.
>
> This struck me as unheroic conduct on the part of the big, strong man who was holding the little boy by the hand. I had contrasted this situation with another which befitted my feelings better: the scene in which Hannibal's father, Hamilcar Barca, made his boy swear before the household altar to take vengeance on the Romans. Ever since that time Hannibal had had a place in my fantasies.

Freud goes on to describe his identification with the Carthaginian general.

> Hannibal and Rome symbolized, in my youthful eyes, the struggle between the tenacity of the Jews and the organization of the Catholic Church. The significance for our emotional life which the anti-Semitic movement has since assumed helped to fix the thoughts and impressions of those earlier days. Thus the desire to go to Rome has in my dream-life become the mask and symbol for a number of warmly cherished wishes, for whose realization one had to work with the tenacity and single-mindedness of the Punic general, though their fulfilment at times seemed as remote as Hannibal's lifelong wish to enter Rome.

Sigmund Freud, considered by many to be the father of psychoanalysis, was deeply inspired by the story of Hannibal.

Not only is Freud's fixation on Hannibal significant in terms of the way he views his relationship with his father, it plays out in his dream life. He mentions that while he and others were more swayed towards the plight of Carthage when learning about the Punic Wars, it is Rome that Freud sees in his dreaming state. Indeed, Hannibal must have had a similar obsession with Rome seeing as he spent many more years focused on conquering Rome than he did living within Carthage's walls.

Robert Frost's "Hannibal"

Robert Frost, arguably one of the greatest American poets to ever live, was also interested in Hannibal, enough to write a poem with his name serving as the title. His book of poetry entitled *West-Running Brook* was published in 1928. It contained his more famous work "Acquainted with the Night," and also this short gem referencing Carthage's greatest military leader.

> "Hannibal"
>
> Was there even a cause too lost,
>
> Ever a cause that was lost too long,
>
> Or that showed with the lapse of time to vain
>
> For the generous tears of youth and song?

Here Frost seems to be meditating on a goal that may be unattainable but still manages to excite enthusiasm. Using "Hannibal" as the title encourages the reader to specifically consider Hannibal's mission. His very name complicates the poem which is phrased as a question. While it would be easy to read the poem with the notion that one should never give up one's dreams, Hannibal's name gives the reader pause. Less harsh than Juvenal, Frost seems to be asking whether or not Hannibal's losses (his country, his safety) were worth what he gave up for glory. Hannibal has lived on in the modern imagination as a symbol of balancing obsessive mission with reason and caution.

Hannibal on Film

The epic nature of the Second Punic War, with its elephants and Roman slaughter, mercenary soldiers and ambush attacks, lends itself to visual reenactment. Directors of major motion pictures and documentaries have been depicting the story of Carthage and Hannibal for decades. Not only are there dozens of fact-based documentaries about Hannibal, a modern Hollywood epic is said to be in development.

Italian Films

Italy has had an interest in depicting Hannibal onscreen since 1914. Giovanni Pastrone's silent film *Cabiria*, which takes place during the Second Punic War and events in Sicily and Carthage, is considered to be a groundbreaking achievement. The film's plot would be considered melodramatic by today's standards and includes a kidnapping of the young female title character, monstrous Carthaginian ceremonies, and even an erupting volcano. The film has been praised by Roger Ebert and Martin Scorsese for its inventiveness. Scorsese goes so far as to assert that Pastrone invented the genre of epic films. Part of what made this film revolutionary was the use of a moving camera as opposed to only relying on a stationary camera. This choice allowed the film

SCHNEIDER.
KNILLING sc.
H. Leutemann. 1866

MODERN SCIENCE AND HANNIBAL'S ROUTE THROUGH THE ALPS

Hannibal's crossing of the Alps has captured the imagination of students of ancient history for thousands of years. Historians have long debated not just how but where Hannibal made his famous crossing. Some scholars argue that Hannibal took a northerly route through two passes, while others think the Carthaginian crossed via a southerly path across the Col de la Traversette, a high mountain pass almost eight thousand feet above sea level. The former director of the Natural History Museum in London, Sir Gavin de Beer, believed Hannibal took the southern path and published a variety of texts throughout the 1950s and 1960s supporting his theory. He studied the ancient writings that detailed Hannibal's march and looked for geographical evidence to back up his claim. Professor Bill Mahaney and an international team of colleagues may have found proof that de Beer was correct. Mahaney took soil samples along the Col de Traversette and found that they contained organic components similar to those found in horse dung. The team also found evidence of clostridia, bacteria found in the intestines of horses and humans. Since there are few mammals that live in the area, Mahaney is confident they will eventually find conclusive evidence to support Hannibal's use of the Col de la Traversette. He hopes to survey the area further looking for items that the passing army may have dropped during their voyage such as weapons, armor, or coins. However, not all scholars agree that Mahaney's search for a smoking gun will yield results. Some steadfastly believe in the northerly route while others, like Patrick Hunt of the Stanford Alpine Archaeology Project, believe the mystery of where Hannibal made his incredible crossing may be impossible to solve.

Opposite: From military strategists to modern scientists, Hannibal's trek through the Alps continues to capture the imagination of mankind.

to deviate from the stagnant viewpoint that other films featured. While the film was pioneering in terms of cinematic art form, it faces the same criticism that many early epics do. Much like D.W. Griffith's *Birth of a Nation*, *Cabiria* seems to serve as a kind of post-war **propaganda**. It was released just after the Italo-Turkish War, in which Italy was victorious in fighting against North African Ottoman provinces. The film focuses on the nobility of Rome's past and portrays the Carthaginians as evil heathens. The film seems to be aimed at inspiring Italians to glorify their past and to see victory as a sort of birthright. Pastrone's vision is interesting, especially considering that Hannibal did manage to sway some Italians to his cause.

Another Italian film that used Hannibal to stir emotions of its viewers was funded by none other than the Italian dictator, Benito Mussolini. In 1937, the propaganda film *Scipio Africanus: The Defeat of Hannibal* was released. It details Scipio Africanus's rise to power and the Battle of Zama as a means of winning support for the fascist invasion of North Africa. Italian soldiers were even used as extras in this motion picture. Again, an Italian movie maker attempted to use the story of Hannibal's downfall to invest national pride in Italian viewers.

The 1959 film *Hannibal* was filmed by Carlo Ludovico Bragaglia, an Italian director, but it was largely financed by Warner Brothers studio. It was promoted as a historical adventure and takes great liberties with the story of Hannibal. In the film, Hannibal's soldiers capture "Sylvia," the daughter of Fabius Maximus. Hannibal and Sylvia fall in love, and some of his troops revolt. The film features scenes depicting the Battle of Cannae as well as representations of Hannibal's wife and child. Though the film is clumsy in its Hollywood version of Hannibal's exploits, it is clear that both Warner Brothers and Bragaglia believed moviegoers were still familiar with the great Carthaginian and captivated by his triumphs.

Contemporary Portrayals

In the last twenty years, Hannibal has been the subject of many modern television documentaries. The History Channel has highlighted Hannibal's life and legend in episodes of series such as *Decisive Battles, Battles BC, Ancients Behaving Badly* and most recently, *Barbarians Rising*, which was executive-produced by Halle Berry and features the actor Nicholas Pinnock as Hannibal. Spike TV's series *Deadliest Warrior* has featured episodes in which the show's creators imagine who would prevail in battle, pitting Hannibal's methods of war versus warriors such as Alexander the Great and Genghis Khan. In 2010, the British Broadcasting Corporation released a series called *On Hannibal's Trail*, which follows three brothers who are attempting to follow Hannibal's route from Spain to Rome via bicycle. These more modern investigations of the legacy of Hannibal seem to be more playful than past contemplations of the legendary general. This may reflect the steady absorption of Hannibal's iconic exploits into the modern consciousness. If these meditations on the Carthaginian aren't entertaining enough, actor Vin Diesel has been working to make a movie about Hannibal's accomplishments for years. The film is currently titled *Hannibal the Conqueror* and is listed as being in development on IMDB.com. In any case, it is clear that Hannibal's legacy lives on in heart, minds, and art of modern citizens.

CHRONOLOGY

247 BCE–183 BCE Lifespan of Hannibal.

221 BCE Hannibal rises to general of Carthage's armies in Spain.

219 BCE Hannibal attacks Saguntum, initiating the Second Punic War.

MARCH 218 BCE Rome declares war on Carthage.

APRIL 218 BCE–MAY 218 BCE Hannibal marches his army towards Italy and crosses the Alps.

NOVEMBER 218 BCE Hannibal wins the battle of Ticinus.

DECEMBER 218 BCE Hannibal wins the battle of Trebia.

217 BCE–218 BCE Hannibal recruits 30,000 Celtic infantry and 4,000 Celtic cavalry.

JUNE 217 BCE Hannibal wins the battle of Lake Trasimene.

AUGUST 216 BCE Hannibal deals Rome its worst defeat ever at the battle of Cannae.

207 BCE Hannibal is cornered in southern Italy.

203 BCE Hannibal is called to defend Carthage against Scipio Africanus.

OCTOBER 202 BCE Scipio Africanus defeats Hannibal at Battle of Zama, ends the Second Punic War.

195 BCE Hannibal flees Carthage to avoid surrender to Rome. Eventually becomes one of the military advisors of King Antiochos in his war against Rome.

CA. 183 BCE King Prusias surrenders Hannibal's location to Rome. Hannibal commits suicide in order to avoid capture.

146 BCE Carthage is destroyed by Rome, ending the Third Punic War.

GLOSSARY

ADAGES Popular sayings.

ARDUOUS Trying; difficult.

ATTRITION Deprivation, loss.

CIRCUS Roman building devoted to chariot racing.

CISTERN Storage container used for holding water.

CONSUL Roman magistrate.

DIGRESSIVE Departing from the main topic.

DIPLOMACY International relations requiring tact.

DUBIOUS Likely to be dishonest.

FLANK Side of a formation.

HULL Main body of a ship.

INCENSED Enraged.

INDEMNITY Compensation.

MARINA Harbor.

MERCENARY Paid professional soldier.

PAPYRUS Ancient form of paper.

POLYTHEISTIC Belief in more than one god.

PREDECESSORS Ancestors.

PROLIFERATED Swift increase.

PROPAGANDA Misleading publicity meant to promote a belief or idea.

PROWESS High level of skill.

PUNITIVE Relating to punishment.

QUINQUEREME Massive ancient warship used to ram enemy vessels.

RAZE Destroy completely.

SATIRE The use of witticisms and comedy to expose faults.

SEAFARING Regularly transporting or traveling by sea.

SEMINAL Important.

STADIA Plural of stadium.

STELAE Upright slab serving as a gravestone.

SUFFETE Carthaginian chief magistrate.

SUPPRESS To put a stop to.

TARIFF Tax.

VELITES Roman light infantrymen.

VEXED Annoyed.

VISCERAL Related to instincts as opposed to intellect.

WAR CHEST Funds used to wage war.

FURTHER INFORMATION

VIDEOS

Engineering An Empire: Carthage

https://www.youtube.com/watch?v=HetYXwtCCho

This documentary examines the rise of Carthage and the engineering that supported the wealthy city-state.

Hannibal: Rome's Worst Nightmare

https://www.youtube.com/watch?v=5y1qF4qud1Q

This docudrama produced by the British Broadcasting Cooperation features reenacted scenes from Hannibal's life based on true events.

The True Story of Hannibal: The History Channel

https://www.youtube.com/watch?v=JU_XtBYeX2o

Watch as historians and scholars analyze Hannibal's rise to power, his astonishing victories against Rome and his eventual defeat by Rome.

WEBSITES

Dickinson College Commentaries: Cornelius Nepos / Life of Hannibal

http://dcc.dickinson.edu/nepos-hannibal/preface

Peruse the history of Carthage and the Punic Wars as derived from ancient Greek and Roman texts at the Dickinson College Commentaries website.

The History Channel: Hannibal

http://www.history.com/topics/ancient-history/hannibal

Read articles and watch videos about Hannibal Barca and his military campaign against Rome on the History Channel's website.

Illustrated History of The Roman Empire

http://www.roman-empire.net/index.html

Discover the history of ancient Rome at this detailed site. Click on 'The Early Republic' to learn about the Punic Wars.

ORGANIZATIONS

UNESCO World Heritage Centre: Archaeological Site of Carthage

http://whc.unesco.org/en/list/37

Learn about the archaeological site of ancient Carthage and all that's being done to protect and preserve the land and its history.

BIBLIOGRAPHY

Carey, Brian Todd, Joshua B. Allfree, and John Cairns. *Hannibal's Last Battle: Zama and the Fall of Carthage*. Yardley, PA: Westholme Publishing, 2008.

Gabriel, Richard A. *Hannibal: The Military Biography of Rome's Greatest Enemy*. Washington, DC: Potomac Books, 2011.

Garland, Robert. *Hannibal*. London: Bristol Classical Press, 2010.

Goldsworthy, Adrian Keith. *The Punic Wars*. London: Cassell, 2000.

Kluth, Andreas. *Hannibal and Me: What History's Greatest Military Strategist Can Teach Us about Success and Failure*. New York: Riverhead Books, 2011.

MacDonald, Eve. *Hannibal: A Hellenistic Life*. New Haven: Yale University Press, 2015.

Mellor, Ronald, and Marni McGee. *The Ancient Roman World*. Oxford: Oxford University Press, 2005.

Miles, Richard. *Carthage Must Be Destroyed: The Rise and Fall of an Ancient Mediterranean Civilization*. London: Allen Lane, 2010.

O'Connell, Robert L. *The Ghosts of Cannae: Hannibal and the Darkest Hour of the Roman Republic*. New York: Random House, 2011.

Prevas, John. *Hannibal Crosses the Alps: The Invasion of Italy and the Punic Wars*. Cambridge, MA: Da Capo Press, 2001. Print.

INDEX

Page numbers in **boldface** are illustrations. Entries in **boldface** are glossary terms.

ABOUT THE AUTHOR

JOEL NEWSOME is a freelance author who has written about a variety of topics including the mythology of elves and minority soldiers who fought in the Civil War. He currently resides in Fort Lauderdale, Florida.